A Candlelight Ecstasy Romance®

"I WISH TO GOD I COULD SEE YOU," SAXON MUTTERED. "COME HERE, IN FRONT OF ME."

Maggie's heart went wild when he leaned forward and cupped her face in his warm, strong hands.

"This is the only way I have of seeing you now," he said quietly. "Do you really mind?"

"No," she whispered. "No, I don't mind."

He caught her by the shoulders, holding her in front of him. His fingers released her and began a journey of discovery that made her tremble with delight. His lips were exquisitely gentle, rubbing against hers with a slight, teasing pressure.

"You taste like a virgin," he whispered, and his lips smiled tenderly against hers. "Are you?"

A CANDLELIGHT ECSTASY ROMANCE ®

DARK SURRENDER

Diana Blayne

A CANDLELIGHT ECSTASY ROMANCE ®

Published by
Dell Publishing Co., Inc.
1 Dag Hammarskjold Plaza
New York, New York 10017

Dell ® TM 681510, Dell Publishing Co., Inc.
Candlelight Ecstasy Romance ® 1,203,540, is a registered
trademark of Dell Publishing Co., Inc.,
New York, New York.

ISBN: 0-440-11833-6

Printed in the United States of America
First printing—October 1983

To Our Readers:

We have been delighted with your enthusiastic response to Candlelight Ecstasy Romances®, and we thank you for the interest you have shown in this exciting series.

In the upcoming months we will continue to present the distinctive sensuous love stories you have come to expect only from Ecstasy. We look forward to bringing you many more books from your favorite authors and also the very finest work from new authors of contemporary romantic fiction.

As always, we are striving to present the unique, absorbing love stories that you enjoy most—books that are more than ordinary romance.

Your suggestions and comments are always welcome. Please write to us at the address below.

Sincerely,

The Editors
Candlelight Romances
1 Dag Hammarskjold Plaza
New York, New York 10017

CHAPTER ONE

Autumn felt good. It made Maggie Sterline's heart quicken to see the bonfires late in the afternoon, to smell the faint scent of powdering leaves mingled with woodsmoke. It brought back haunting tales of hobgoblins and magic and Indian campfires. Of course, the leaves in south Georgia were nothing like the glory in the northern end of the state, where ghostly mountains lifted their smooth peaks to be dotted with gold-and-red dabs of color against sapphire canvas that was the autumn sky. But it was much the same in other ways. The Indians had once lived in this part of her native state, too, Maggie thought, and the moccasined feet of the Lower Creeks had left their imprints in local history. There were arrowheads and bits of pottery all around Defiance testifying to that early occupation.

Maggie had always liked the town's name: Defiance. It sounded as if it liked impossible odds, and if Saxon Tremayne caught up with her, she'd need some defiance. Some hope.

The thought of the big man made her shudder. She'd come very close to falling in love with Saxon in those weeks she'd spent in his company while she'd worked on an in-depth photo feature about the industrial giant for the regional magazine she'd worked for in South Carolina. It had been great fun. And she'd only been dimly aware that Kerry Smith was working on an exposé about some local cotton mill causing brown lung. If only she'd paid attention!

She perched herself on the edge of her cluttered desk. Maggie was a good-looking young brunette of twenty-six; not pretty, but slender and attractive, from her high firm breasts to her small waist and narrow hips. She had good legs, too, but today she'd wrapped them in long fashionable boots under a colorful gray-and-red plaid skirt over which she wore a white blouse and a knitted gray vest. She looked trendy, but not flashy, and the newspaper's owner, Ernie Wilson, liked the touch of class she lent to his modest operation—or so he said. The owner of *The Defiant Banner* had known Maggie's family since his grandfather bought the newspaper, and he was sometimes more of an uncle than an employer. He hadn't even asked questions when Maggie had come into his office looking for a job, her face drawn and haggard, her jade-green eyes hunted and afraid. Ernie Wilson never asked questions, and Maggie assumed it was because he had such a knack for reading minds.

She'd needed the job desperately. More than a means of support, it had meant a refuge from the furious textile magnate who'd blamed her for selling him out for the sake of a story. His subsequent battle with the environmental people and his plant's labor union had been a direct consequence of the accusing front-page story about the lung-damaging capabilities of his plant and his carelessness in not correcting the situation. In fact, the modifications to update the plant and install a new system to control the damaging cotton dust had been planned and were well on their way to being implemented. But the story didn't make mention of that fact; it made it seem as if Saxon Tremayne was a money-mad businessman who put profits above safety. And he'd blamed Maggie for that piece of damning fiction. He'd judged her guilty without giving her the benefit of the doubt or an opportunity to tell him her side of it. He'd promised only retribution for her betrayal, and Saxon Tremayne was a man of his word. It was worth its weight in diamonds, and in the South Carolina textile town of Jarrettsville, it was law.

Maggie hadn't wanted to leave the graceful little town. She was innocent, and if he'd given her half a chance, she might have proved it to him. But he hadn't been in a listening mood the day the story broke. His voice had bellowed at her over the phone, deep and slow and as cold as a mortuary. He'd cut her off before she could put the blame on a mix-up over by-lines, promising reprisals in that cutting tone he used best in a temper. He never raised his voice, but it was worse than being yelled at.

The worst thing of all was that her heart, so long untouched, had finally been his for the taking. She'd learned to love the big man in the brief period she'd spent with him, and if she'd just had a little more time, she might have been able to catch his eye. He'd been friendly, cooperative. But not once had he touched her or looked at her in any intimate way. People said he was still grieving for his late wife. But nothing he'd told Maggie gave the impression that

11

he'd felt anything at all for the woman who'd shared his bed and board for eighteen years. Maggie had wondered at the time if he was capable of deep emotions. He seemed to be a loner, involved deeply in business but only casually interested in his family. There wasn't much of that either, she knew: a stepbrother, a mother, and a few scattered cousins whom he barely acknowledged. She didn't even know where his family lived.

"Daydreaming again?" a light, teasing voice whispered at her ear.

Her dark-lashed eyes flew open, their emerald-green depths brilliant enough to shock as she met Eve's dancing gray ones.

"Sorry," Maggie murmured sheepishly, and blushed. "I was just going over some notes in my mind."

"About how to help the firemen raise enough funds to buy that new turnout gear Harry's got his heart set on?" Eve grinned. "Come on, Maggie, don't hold out on me. Who's caught your eye?"

Maggie smiled mysteriously. "A great, hulking creature with eyes like a tiger's—tawny and deep-set and mysterious," she replied, exaggerating only a little. "No, really, I was trying to decide which of the city commission candidates to call first for an interview." She sighed. "It's going to take me two weeks to wrap up this race." She moaned. "Pictures, interviews—and none of them will hit the issues on the head. I'm so *tired* of having men tell me they're running for office because the city *needs* them. My gosh, Eve, if they really cared about the city, at least four of them would never run for office in it!"

Eve patted the taller woman's shoulder. "There, there," she murmured. "It's all those years you spent working for a magazine that's done this to you. You'll get used to it."

"Why won't they answer my questions?" she asked wearily.

"Because the way you get elected in Defiance is to say as little about yourself as possible. The less the voters know," she whispered conspiratorially, "the more of them will vote for you."

Maggie stared at the ceiling, as if she expected to find answers hanging from it. "Dad warned me not to go to college in South Carolina," she murmured. "That really was my worst mistake. I should have stayed in Defiance and gone into local politics."

"Run for office," Eve encouraged her. "I'll vote for you."

Maggie stretched lazily. "Personally I'm voting for Thomas Jefferson in this election."

"He's dead," Eve pointed out.

"Well, I won't hold that against him," Maggie said straight-faced. She ran a hand through her dark hair impatiently. "I guess I'd better hit the road. I'll swing by Jake Henderson's place and take a picture of that giant cabbage he's grown while I'm out. Have I got anything pending?"

Eve checked the big calendar on the wall, scribbled all over with a big red pen, and shook her head. "A luncheon tomorrow when they're giving out those student awards at Rotary, that's all."

"Okay." Maggie grabbed up her thirty-five millimeter camera and an extra roll of film along with her purse and paused at the door. "Call if you need me."

"I'll come myself," Eve promised with a wry glance at the doorway leading into the makeup room. She raised her voice above the soft humming sound coming from the computer in the next office. "I need a break, what with all the hard work I do around here that goes unappreciated!"

A tall, gray-haired man with a slight paunch came to the door, scissors and a galley proof in his hand.

"If you want to do some work, Miss Johns," he told Eve, "get in here and start pasting up. I've got the front page and the editorial page done and twelve more waiting while you pass the time with Miss Big-city Journalist there."

"I don't associate with you backwoods journalists," Maggie informed him haughtily. "And I fully expect to get a Pulitzer with my fine feature on Mr. Henderson's twenty-five-pound cabbage that he raised from a tiny seed in his garden."

Ernie Wilson stared at her unblinkingly. It was the look he used on Tuesday, when they were making up the final pages and they were sitting on the deadline for the printers. It was a cross between despair, exasperation, and the threat of imminent alcoholism. It spoke volumes.

"Bye," Maggie said quickly. With a wink at Eve she dashed out the door.

Professor Anthony Sterline was relaxing in the small living room with his afternoon paper when Maggie dragged into the house, kicking off her shoes in the hall.

"I'm here," she called.

"About time," her father replied dryly. "You're an hour late. Not that I expected you early, since it's Tuesday."

"I'll never get used to standing on my feet all day while we make up that . . . paper." She sighed, joining her father on the sofa. She leaned back and closed her eyes. "Oh, if supper would only cook itself."

"It has," came the amused reply. "Lisa's home."

Maggie's eyes flew open. "Already? I thought she'd be much later."

"Her flight was canceled, so she traded places with one of the other stewardesses and came home early. She's got engaged."

"Engaged? I didn't even know she was dating anyone," Maggie said with considerable interest.

"Randy Steele. Didn't she mention him? The family lives in Jarrettsville. Very well-to-do, she says," he said.

Steele. Steele. Somewhere in the back of Maggie's tired brain that name ran bells. But she couldn't quite place it. But Jarrettsville was one place she'd never forget.

"Maggie!" her sister cried suddenly, flinging herself through the door and onto her taller sister's prone body with a gleeful laugh. Lisa was fair and green-eyed, and nobody who saw them together would have suspected they were sisters. Lisa's features were delicate and sharp, where Maggie's were more muted. Lisa was small-boned, and Maggie was tall and statuesque. But the one thing they did share was the color of their eyes—the same bright jade-green of their father's eyes, unmistakable.

15

They began to talk all at once, exchanging greetings, asking questions, until the excitement faded for a minute.

"Dad says you're engaged," Maggie ventured.

"Tattletale," the shorter woman told her father, sticking her tongue out at him. "I wanted to surprise her. He's gorgeous," she added with a sigh. "Tall and sexy—and rich too—although that's not why I said I'd marry him. I'm so in love, it hurts," she added solemnly. "I never dreamed it would happen to me, and certainly not like lightning striking. We've only been dating for a month."

"When have you set the date?"

Lisa looked uncomfortable. "That's the hitch. Randy won't set the date until he decides what to do about his home problems. I'm going to fly up there this weekend and meet his mother and brother. I'd like very much to have you go with me. I'm going to need some support."

It was beginning to sound like a play. Maggie stared at her sister. "Support?" she prodded gently.

Lisa sat down in the armchair across from the sofa and looked preoccupied. "Randy's brother is blind," she said quietly. "There's only him and his mother in the big house in Jarrettsville, and Randy doesn't feel right about marrying and leaving the responsibility for his brother with his mother."

"A commendable attitude," their father said with an approving nod. "But is the brother a total invalid?"

"I get the feeling," Lisa said slowly, "that he's something of a tiger. He was a high-powered businessman before his accident, always on the go. Now he's just not able to live that fast anymore, and he's bitter about it." Lisa studied her pale pink-tipped fingers. "Randy says he won't even leave the house. He won't learn Braille, he won't get a Seeing Eye dog, he won't even try to adjust to it!"

Professor Sterline ran a restless hand over his thinning gray hair. "Perhaps it's just taking him a little time to adjust," he remarked, leaning forward. "I had a student in my history class who was like that. Once he was able to accept his blindness, he progressed rapidly."

"You don't understand, Dad," Lisa said gently. "Hawk's been blind for eight months."

"Hawk? Odd name," her father observed.

"It's a nickname, but I've never heard Randy call him anything else," Lisa said with a wry smile. "Anyway it's not as if the accident just happened or anything. And he's gone through half a dozen nurses. Randy says he's a holy terror."

"A lion with a thorn in his paw," Maggie corrected gently, feeling a strange kinship with the unknown blind man. Her own trauma had begun about that same length of time ago. "He just needs someone to pull it out."

"How are you with a pair of tweezers?" Lisa teased. "You will come, won't you? Mrs. Steele's looking forward to meeting you."

"I'm not sure if my life insurance covers lions," came the dry reply. "And my memories of Jarrettsville are rather . . . unpleasant."

"We'll carry a chair and a whip to protect us from

17

Hawk," Lisa promised. "But I didn't know you'd ever been to Jarrettsville. . . ."

"What is his mother like?" Maggie asked, eager to change the subject.

"Long-suffering and patient, he says," her sister told her with a smile. "I've never met her. Randy says the house sits right on the edge of the Blue Ridge Mountain foothills, surrounded by huge live oaks. It was a plantation during the Civil War."

"It does sound interesting," Professor Sterline remarked, his eyes lighting up at any mention of his subject. "Magnolia Gardens is in South Carolina, you know, and there's a fascinating story behind it. It seems that . . ."

The girls weren't in time to stop him, so they sat quietly and listened with grave courtesy while Professor Sterline gave them the long history of the Civil War in South Carolina. Maggie didn't usually hear many of his lectures since she'd moved into her own apartment; she spent the night only when her sister was in town so the three of them could have some time together.

That night Maggie lay awake a long time, her mind full of Saxon Tremayne. The trip back to South Carolina was one she'd rather not have made, but she couldn't deny Lisa that small sacrifice. Besides, if Saxon hadn't come after her head in eight months, it was unlikely that he'd still be in the mood for retribution.

That had disappointed her in one minor way. She'd wanted him to come after her—for any reason, even revenge. In her mind she could see those tawny eyes watching her, studying her, in a face as broad and tanned as a Roman's, his size setting him apart as much as his air of authority. He was a striking man: rugged, commanding, with a voice like rich, dark velvet when he spoke softly. Not a day had gone by that she hadn't thought about him, missed him, wondered if he'd forgiven her for what he'd thought she'd done. If only she could write and explain. Perhaps now that his black temper had cooled, she could reason with him, tell him the truth. But if he was still angry, writing to him could be a monumental mistake. She'd never talked about her hometown; there had never been the opportunity. He knew she was from Georgia, but not where, and she was faintly glad. Saxon never hesitated to use his power. He wouldn't have batted an eye at buying out the newspaper to fire her. And there were other, less pleasant ways he could have chosen to get even with her.

She rolled over, burying her hot face in the cool pillow. Perhaps it was best this way. What did she have in common with a millionaire, after all? Even if she'd caught Saxon's eye, he'd probably have had no use for her past his bedroom. He wasn't a man to form permanent relationships; his mind was devoted entirely to business. If only she could forget.

This trip with Lisa would take her mind off it at least. And certainly being around Randy's fiery brother would keep her occupied. She smiled secretly. Hawk sounded like the bird of prey from which his nickname undoubtedly came, sharp and deadly. She was intrigued already by Lisa's description of him. How dreadful to have had so much, and lose it through blindness. She wondered idly if she might be

19

able to get through that layer of fierce bitterness and help the poor lion find peace.

It was a tempting thought. She closed her eyes on it and drifted slowly off to sleep.

CHAPTER TWO

Randolph Steele was every bit the dish Lisa had described. He was tall, whipcord slim, with dark hair and an olive complexion, and blue eyes under impossibly thick eyelashes. He had a live-wire personality, and it was obvious from the moment he met them at the Greenville airport that Lisa had his whole heart.

He kissed her with gusto, then stood back to study her petite figure with eyes that spoke volumes before he turned to extend a hand to Maggie.

"You must be the big sister," he said. "As you have probably already deduced, I am the fiancé."

"I had a sneaking hunch you weren't a total stranger," Maggie replied, giving his hand a firm warm shake. "Nice to meet you."

"Maggie's a reporter, you know," Lisa burst out enthusiastically. "She writes for our local paper!"

"Will you be quiet?" Maggie groaned, whirling around in frustrated embarrassment with her hands clasped behind her head. "You know I don't like to talk about what I do!"

"Your guilty secret is safe with me," Randy replied, leading them out to the parking lot with a suitcase in either hand. "And, kidding aside, you'd better keep it a secret from Hawk. He hates reporters."

"Was your mother frightened by one before she gave birth to him?" Maggie asked with a grin.

Randy laughed at that. "Not my mother. Hawk is my stepbrother. In a sense he and his father married me and my mother. Steele Manor was mother's, of course, but Hawk controls the family finances. Mother is a dear, but a bit frivolous, and she has no business head."

"Your stepbrother must be pretty smart," Lisa said.

"Brilliant," Randy corrected. He paused beside an elegant deep burgundy Lincoln town car and after the bags had been safely stored in the trunk, asked the women to come inside—Lisa on the passenger side and Maggie in the back—before he slid in under the wheel.

"What does he do?" Lisa asked.

"He's a businessman. Or he was," Randy corrected sadly. "When his father died, he took over all the family holdings, and there were a lot of them. He was constantly on the move up until the accident."

Lisa reached out and caught Randy's free hand as he pulled the car out into traffic and headed it out of Greenville. Maggie, who'd only been to Greenville once before, was fascinated by the blend of historical buildings and modern ones, the sprawling downtown mall and the unusual street signs as well as the surprising small-town look of the downtown area, all set against the distant backdrop of the Blue Ridge Mountains.

"What kind of business is the family in?" Maggie

asked politely, her eyes roving everywhere as they moved out of town.

"Textiles," Randy replied, shooting a smile and a wink toward Lisa.

"What a coincidence," Lisa cooed. "Maggie used to write about them a lot in her old job, before she came home. She was a—"

"Do shut up, darling," Maggie told her younger sister with a sweet smile, "or I'll tape up your mouth. Randy doesn't want to hear about my whole history. I'm sure he's much more interested in yours."

Besides, she added silently, *if his people are in textiles and he learns why I left Jarrettsville, he might know Saxon Tremayne and let it slip. And that kind of trouble I don't need!*

"You're so modest," Lisa complained. "Why don't you want people to know you write? Besides, Randy's family . . . almost," she added shyly.

He squeezed her hand. "Very almost. All we have to do is figure a way out of this mess my family's in." He sighed. "I just can't leave mother here with Hawk. It would be like sacrificing her. His temper was always formidable, but since the accident he's been like a wild man. One nurse left the house at three o'clock in the morning in her nightgown. In her nightgown! The police stopped her, of course, and wanted an explanation. They called the house, and we cleared up the misunderstanding. Hawk gets violent headaches sometimes at night, he went to ask her for an injection, and she thought he wanted something quite different." He laughed shortly. "Anyway it embarrassed mother to tears. She

23

couldn't face her garden club the next day, and she's hardly been out of the house since."

Mrs. Steele sounded like a sparrow turned loose in a cage with an eagle. How hard it must be for her to live with her volatile stepson and retain her sanity, Maggie thought.

"Couldn't you find a former combat nurse?" Lisa teased.

"We did, don't laugh," he replied with a wicked smile. "A crusty old ex-lieutenant who'd been in the Wacs. She lasted a week. You think I'm joking. When you meet Hawk, you'll see that I'm not."

"Is there any hope that they might be able to restore his sight surgically?" Maggie asked gently.

"Not really. It would be much too dangerous. Hawk won't even talk about it."

"How did it happen?" Maggie asked softly.

"Hawk served two tours in Vietnam. He earned that nickname because he never missed with an M1 rifle. It's rather ironic that he didn't lose his sight over there when he caught the shrapnel in his head. The doctor explained to me that the shrapnel had lodged near the base of the frontal lobe of his brain, but didn't impair him in any way until it was dislodged eight months ago in that wreck and blinded him. The best he can hope for now is that the shrapnel will someday shift again and relieve the pressure on his optic nerve." Randy sighed. "If he hadn't been in such a temper, it never would have happened. He has monumental control usually. But he'd had a hell of a lot of pressure, what with the newspaper story and the union going out on a wildcat strike, and then the ultimatum by the environmental people. He'd just called a meeting on it and was rushing to the plant on a rain-slick highway when the car went into a skid." He shrugged. "The problem solved itself, of course, when the union and the state people realized that the solution was almost in operation. A tempest in a teapot, as they say. A quiet disaster."

Scandal. Environmental people. Story. Maggie went rigid in the backseat.

"Funny," Lisa murmured. "Maggie wrote a story about some textile company, didn't you, Maggie? Dad said something about it in passing. . . ."

Randy laughed and shook his head as he turned into a side road. "Maggie wouldn't write that kind of story, I don't think. My God, Hawk went right through the ceiling over it. It was a pack of lies, and I'll never know how it got into print. Two reporters were fired over it, as I recall, but the main culprit got away. Hawk would have crucified her if he hadn't been blinded. He was out for blood."

Maggie felt as if she were smothering—choking, dying. It was like some horrible dream, and she couldn't wake up from it.

"What is your stepbrother's name?" Maggie asked in a husky whisper. "His real name?"

"Hawk? His name is Saxon," Randy told her matter-of-factly. "Saxon Tremayne."

Maggie's breath seemed to trap itself in her throat, so that it could neither back up nor go forward. She wanted to throw herself out of the car, to run, to escape. But the Lincoln was already winding up the long paved driveway to the Steeles' Victorian home, fronted by a garden that must have been glorious in the spring.

"Your mother's name . . . isn't Steele," Maggie said weakly.

"No, it's Tremayne," Randy agreed, missing the panic in his green-eyed passenger's face. "I kept my father's name, so lots of people assume that hers is still Steele too. What do you think of my home, darling?" he asked Lisa, who was equally unaware of Maggie's buried terrors.

"I love it," Lisa sighed dreamily, studying the front of the massive house with its gingerbread woodwork, long front porch with white furniture, and neatly trimmed surrounding shrubs and trees.

"I hoped you would," he murmured softly.

A dainty little blond maid opened the door for them.

"Is mother home, Grace?" Randy asked her with a pleasant smile.

"Mrs. Tremayne is in the living room, sir," came the sweet reply, joined by a wistful glance as she watched him enter the wide hall with Lisa on his arm.

"Thanks," he murmured, leading the women to the entrance of the spacious Early American–style room with champagne-colored draperies and a huge stone fireplace with two high-backed chairs facing it. A fire was glowing brightly in the hearth, warming the room against the chill of autumn.

Maggie's hunted eyes roamed around as she searched wildly for a way to go home. She couldn't stay here. Not now.

Sandra Tremayne rose as they entered the room, a small, thin little woman with clouds of tinted blond hair and eyes the gray of a winter sky. She stood up to envelop her tall son in her arms, a cloud of delicious perfume drifting around her like the pale blue dress she was wearing with her white pearls.

"You must be Lisa," she said softly after she'd welcomed Randy, smiling shyly at the young woman at his side.

"I am," Lisa said, smiling back. "Randy's told me so much about you, I couldn't wait to meet you. And I do love your home."

"I'm fond of it, too, especially in the spring. And this must be Maggie," she added with a smile in the brunette's direction.

Maggie extended her hand and found it gripped warmly. "I'm glad to meet you," she replied courteously.

"I've looked forward to this," Sandra confided. "Your rooms are all ready for you, and—"

"I can't stay," Maggie blurted out, ignoring Lisa's shocked expression. "I just remembered, I'd promised to cover a story tonight, and I really can't go back on my word. I'll have to fly back, and perhaps I can come back down tomorrow," she said in a panicky tone, her voice rising. "Randy, would you mind driving me back to the airport? Or if not, I can get a cab. . . . I'm so sorry," she added quickly, thinking, *I'm going to make it, I'm going to get away before Saxon knows I'm here, before—*

"Surely you aren't leaving when you've only just arrived?" came a deep unmistakable voice from an armchair near the hearth, one of two with their backs to the hall.

Maggie had heard that velvety voice in her dreams. She'd missed it, feared it, agonized over it in

27

the past several months. And now all her worst fears had come to pass. She'd run away, but fate had caught her and flung her back in Saxon's path with a relentless flick of its cruel hand. It was too late to run anymore.

Saxon stood up slowly, as big and imposing as she remembered him. He seemed a little paler—his shaggy dark hair was in need of a trim—but basically he was the same man.

He held on to the back of the chair with a big broad-fingered hand, a ruby ring glittering on a little finger, and stared in the direction of the voices. He wasn't wearing dark glasses, and he wasn't carrying a cane. And all his scars, like Maggie's, seemed to be beneath the exterior.

"H-hello, Mr. Tremayne," Maggie said unsteadily, wishing she had the back of a chair for support.

"Come here," he said without preamble, while three pairs of eyes watched the byplay, fascinated.

Licking her dry lips, Maggie walked gingerly to his chair and stopped just a yard away from him.

"You're not afraid of the blind man, are you?" he asked with a bitter laugh.

"Don't . . ." she whispered shakily, her eyes running over his broad, leonine face hungrily.

"Saxon . . ." his stepmother began nervously.

"You didn't recognize the name?" Saxon asked, raising his voice. "Surely I've cursed it enough! Maggie Sterline. Sterline, dammit!"

Randy whistled through his teeth, tossing a sympathetic look toward Maggie. "I thought the name sounded familiar." He groaned, drawing Lisa close. "Oh, Lord, love, we're in for it now."

28

"Poor Maggie," Lisa murmured, aching for her sister. "If only I'd known. She never said anything to me!"

"She probably didn't connect Hawk with Saxon," Randy said, sighing. "I never called him by name around you either. What a hell of a coincidence."

"Here on a visit, Miss Sterline?" Saxon asked her, venom in his deep voice, in the tawny, sightless eyes. "I hope you packed a bag, because you're staying for a while."

"I . . . am?" she echoed weakly. She wasn't easily intimidated, but there was something in Saxon Tremayne that demanded obedience, and she gave it.

"You sound nervous, Maggie," he said, a giant cat playing with its prey. "Don't panic. It's all worked itself out, and I've got bigger things on my mind than stripping the skin from your lovely body. Pull up a chair and sit down. Randy, Mother . . . close the door on your way out," he added pointedly—not asking, telling.

Randy and Mrs. Tremayne visibly relaxed, and Lisa sighed thankfully. They slipped out the door, closing it gently behind them.

Saxon sat back down in his chair, and Maggie perched on just the edge of the other one, watching him. She couldn't help noticing how the faint gold specks in his black smoking jacket brought out the gold in his tawny eyes; how the fabric stretched sensuously over his massive chest, which tapered to a flat stomach and broad, powerful thighs. He was forty, but it didn't show in that athletic body; only in the silvering at his temples and the new lines in his hard face.

"Ironic, isn't it?" he asked shortly. "Your sister and my stepbrother."

"Are you going to break them up?" she asked quietly.

"That depends on you, honey," he said in a voice she didn't like. "Randy can't buy a shoelace without my signature until he reaches twenty-five. That's two more years. Do you think they can wait that long?"

"That would be cruel. . . ."

"I'm a cruel man," he said curtly. "Women like you have made me wary. Why did you come here?" he added bluntly.

"I didn't know who you were," she replied simply.

"You didn't connect Steele and Tremayne, I gather? I don't suppose I ever mentioned it when we were together." He leaned back, his face going even harder in memory. "I was fascinated by you, Little Miss Journalist, did you know that? I could look at you and ache all over."

She gaped at him. She'd never realized he felt anything but courtesy for her.

"Tongue-tied?" he growled. "Don't let your imagination loose. I was attracted, I'd have liked to get you into my bed for a night or two, but that was as far as it went. Reporters weren't my cup of tea even before you sold me out to your scandal sheet."

"I didn't!" she protested, sitting straighter.

"Oh, hell, I don't even care anymore," he ground out. "It's too late for all that. I'm blind."

She closed her eyes on the flat statement. Blind. Blind. It echoed in her mind like a chant. "I'm sorry," she managed.

"Thank you," he replied coolly. "That helps a hell of a lot."

"I didn't make the roads slick," she cried.

"You wrote the story."

"No, I didn't, I swear I didn't; it was a mixup in the by-lines," she said, trying desperately to convince him.

"I hope you don't expect me to buy that," he replied. He drew a cigarette from his pocket and lighted it as smoothly as a sighted person; he was hardly fumbling at all, Maggie thought.

"You do that . . . very well," she remarked.

"The first time, I set fire to my sleeve," he recalled with a bitter laugh. "But eventually I got the hang of it."

"If there's anything I can do . . ." she began helplessly.

"Oh, there is," he replied smoothly. "Very definitely there is. You can stay for a few weeks, Miss Sterline. You can share this travesty of living with me until I'm convinced you're genuinely repentant."

She chewed on her lower lip. "A whipping boy?" she asked with dignity.

"A companion," he growled. "I need someone to lead me around, haven't you noticed?"

"You had a nurse. . . ."

"Had is right. Yes or no? But if you say no," he added darkly, "I'll forbid the marriage and cut Randy off without a single dime. That wouldn't endear you to your sister, would it?"

"What will it accomplish to keep me here?" she asked uncertainly.

"Quite a lot," he said, his tawny eyes glittering

menacingly across the few feet in her direction. "I owe you, honey. You can't imagine how much I owe you until you see how I have to live from day to day, through the endless nights, with my mind on fire with pain. I want you to see what you accomplished with that damned story you betrayed me for!"

"I didn't betray you!" she cried.

"Can't you even tell the truth when you're caught red-handed?" he asked with disgust in his tone. "My God, why hide behind excuses that won't hold water? Don't you think I checked? They said there was no mix-up—that the picture was yours, and the by-line. The man you accused of writing the damned story was the one who denied it to my face."

"Because you probably went storming into the office and backed him up against a wall," she accused. "Kerry was just a boy!"

"More like a rabbit," he scoffed. "He could barely talk at all."

"If you hate me so much, why do you want me here?" she asked wearily.

"Maybe I'm lonely," he said curtly. "Trapped. Tired of being patronized and pacified and pandered to. Tired of nurses who are too nervous or too belligerent to do me any good." He shifted restlessly, and his eyes closed momentarily. "When Randy told me his fiancée's last name was Sterline, I asked about her family. He mentioned you. It was Christmas, so it was a simple matter to lead him into inviting you with Lisa. I want you with me. You're going to be my eyes for a few weeks. Apart from everything else you might consider that you owe me at least that much—regardless of where the blame lies," he added when she started to speak. His huge shoulders lifted and fell. "I was stupid enough to believe I was the subject of a feature, not a character assassination."

Her eyes washed over him like rain, drinking him. Could she bear being in the same house with this man even for that short time? she wondered. Watching him, seeing him like this, hating his blindness and blaming herself for her small part in it. . . .

"I'll be your eyes," she said finally, in her soft quiet voice, and she saw him visibly relax. "For a while. But I may do you more harm than good, the way you feel about me."

"You don't know how I feel, honey," he returned quietly, crossing one long leg over the other. "If it comes right down to it, I'm not all that sure myself. I've spent months blaming you for everything that's happened, because hatred is a powerful motivation for survival and I needed it. I still need it, in a sense. But I'll try to keep my resentments under control. It's . . . hard for me," he said hesitantly, "being like this. I'm not used to feeling . . . vulnerable."

He meant helpless, she knew, but he couldn't manage the word. It was like weakness, to admit it.

"At least two nurses would testify in court that you aren't vulnerable," she reminded him with a smile he couldn't see.

His dark, heavy eyebrows went straight up. "The night runner and the drill sergeant?" he asked innocently.

She laughed out loud, in spite of herself. "Is that what you called them?"

He shook his head. "I had Randy describe the runaway. He said it was pure conceit on her part if

33

she thought I'd brave her bed, even out of desperation. And the drill sergeant . . . my God, I got tired of being ordered to drink my split-pea soup! Have you ever eaten hospital split-pea soup? That's what hers tasted like—no salt, no seasoning, no peas. Just thick, hot water with a drop of flavoring."

"How about the others?" she asked.

"A few assorted spinsters with Jane Eyre complexes," he said, dismissing them. "How can any woman expect a blind man to fall in love with her on sight? I'd have to feel them to do that, and I don't know many who'd take to being Brailled physically by a stranger. Would you?" he asked suddenly.

She flushed. "You know what I look like," she hedged.

"It's been eight months," he reminded her. "You may have gained weight, or lost it."

He'd teased her like this once before, when she'd been doing the interview, and it had promoted a closeness between them that she had had hopes for. But now she couldn't help but be wary of him after what he'd said. He might be trying to make her vulnerable just to get even with her for what he believed she'd done, and she didn't dare drop her guard.

"I might contaminate you," she returned with a sting in her voice.

"Temper, temper," he said with a maddening smile.

"You're a pirate," she grumbled.

"With patches over both eyes?" he baited.

"I don't want to stay here!" she burst out suddenly, as she realized the predicament she might find herself in with him.

"But you're going to," he said calmly. He shifted in the big chair, uncrossing his legs. "Would you like to go on salary?" he added. "We can call you a nurse-companion and I'll pay you what the nurses got. You can tell your father I'm hiring you."

"I have a job too," she said quickly, "with our local newspaper."

"You're taking a leave of absence for the next two weeks," he replied.

"My boss won't give me a leave of absence . . ." she began.

"He will if I tell him to," he replied with biting confidence, his whole look arrogant. "If he says no, I'll pay off the mortgage on his paper and fire him."

"How do you know he's got one to pay off?" she returned hotly.

One corner of his mouth went up. "Times are hard, honey, and unless he's thrown in with a combine, he probably has hell keeping the doors open. There's a mortgage."

She couldn't believe that he'd go to those lengths, but it was in every ruthless line of his broad face. He'd decided that he wanted her company, and he was going to get it no matter what lengths he had to go to. She understood now why he was so rich. It had been inevitable, with that raw, driving force in him.

"I'd rather you let me go back home and sent me letter bombs and threatening notes," she replied quietly.

"And I'd rather you stayed. So would your sister,

35

I imagine," he added, reminding her of what he'd threatened earlier.

"Mr. Tremayne—"

"Go and tell the others they can come back in now," he said, ignoring the thought she was trying to voice. He looked weary all of a sudden, and one big hand rubbed at his eyes, as if they pained him.

"I'll have to call my father, and my boss," she began.

"Go ahead."

"Are you sure this is a good idea?" she asked very gently.

"I'd like to meet your sister, if you'd ever go and bring her here," he said impatiently. "And put this out for me," he added, holding the half-finished cigarette out in front of him.

"You don't want a companion, you want slave labor," she grumbled. But she took the cigarette and crushed it out in the ashtray beside his chair. "And to think, before I knew who you were, I actually felt sorry for you. Sorry! I might as well weep for a hungry lion!" she muttered.

He laughed softly, as if the words delighted him. "Go on."

"Yes, sir, Mr. Tremayne," she grumbled on her way out.

All three of them were sitting on the long sofa in the front entrance, as if they were afraid to move too far away because they might miss hearing her scream for help.

"It's all right," Maggie told them, watching with hidden amusement the way they got to their feet.

36

"You're still in one piece," Randy said, breathing a sigh of relief. "My gosh, I'm sorry I let you walk into that, but I had no idea who you were. I didn't even connect it."

"Lisa hadn't told us that you wrote, dear," Sandra Tremayne added gently, her eyes compassionate, not resentful as Maggie had feared they would be after her identity was revealed.

"I'm so sorry about Saxon—Mr. Tremayne," Maggie said earnestly, and the guilt was in her whole look. "It was a mix-up in the by-lines. What I did was a feature story, but the by-lines were switched, and I got the blame for what one of the new reporters had done on brown lung. I had too much respect for Mr. Tremayne to pull an underhanded stunt like that on him. I'm aware that some journalists don't think twice about how they get a story, but I'm not one of them. I hope you believe that, even if he won't."

"I do," Lisa said gently, moving forward to hug her older sister. "I've known you all my life, remember?"

Maggie smiled, her voice wavering as she replied, "Yes, love, I know."

"Nobody's blaming you," Randy said quietly. "Hawk's had a rough time, and he can't come to grips with what's happened. But I know, too, that it could have happened anytime. He could have just as well been on his way to buy gas, or eat out. And for what it's worth, I think Lisa knows you well enough to vouch for you."

"Has he thrown you out?" Sandra asked, genuinely concerned. "I really won't stand for that, you

37

know, it is still my home, and you're very welcome to stay."

"No, he didn't throw me out," Maggie said with a quiet smile. "Quite the opposite. I'm going to be his eyes for a few weeks."

"Or . . . ?" Randy asked knowingly.

Maggie smiled back in spite of herself. "Or he'll buy my employer's newspaper and fire him, he said."

"He probably meant it," Randy agreed with a heavy sigh. "He's paying you for the dubious honor, I hope? I imagine you have bills to handle just like everyone else."

"I have, and he is," Maggie agreed, stretching wearily. "At least he isn't having me stuffed and mounted. That's something. And I think I truly understand how he feels." Her eyes grew sad. "What a tragic thing to have happened. It hasn't been easy for him, I'm sure, as active and involved as he was. And to never get out at all. . . . Why won't he?" she asked.

Randy's lips made a thin line. "He won't be led around like a dumb animal, he says," he told her. "That's the excuse I get anyway. We've both offered. He won't let us help him."

"He may let me," Maggie said thoughtfully. "As long as he thinks I'm being ordered to, at least," she added with a grin.

"And that," Sandra Tremayne told her son, "is why women will rule the world someday. We let you believe you have the ideas, but actually they're all ours. Right, girls?"

"Right," Maggie and Lisa chorused.

Randy only sighed. "Shall we go back in?"

"He wants to meet Lisa," Maggie murmured as

Randy opened the door, and Lisa hesitated, but her sister grabbed her hand and dragged her over to the big high-backed chair.

"Mr. Tremayne, this is Lisa," Maggie said, placing her sister's hand in his big one.

He could be charming when he wanted to—and this, Maggie thought, was one of those times. "I'm very pleased to meet my future sister-in-law," he said with a voice like velvet, and a smile. "What does she look like, Maggie? Like you? Or is she fair?"

"She has short green hair and freckles," Maggie said helpfully. "Oh, and a wart on her left cheek."

He scowled, looking more intimidating than ever in his darkness, his bigness. "There went your Christmas bonus, Snow White," he told Maggie.

She laughed in spite of herself. He looked so ferocious. "She's very fair," she said relenting. "Not quite as tall as I am, much better figure than mine, with green eyes and delicate features. All right?"

"You're insolent, miss," he accused.

"Yes, sir," she agreed, winking at Lisa.

"Now I understand why Lisa is an airline hostess," he remarked. "She does it to get away from you."

"hat was unkind," Maggie murmured.

"nd probably true. You're both probably tired from the trip. Why don't you rest for a while?" he added courteously. "Mother, are the rooms ready?"

"Yes, Saxon," Sandra assured him, relief showing in every soft line of her face. "Come with me and I'll show you upstairs. Can I have the maids bring you anything, dear?" she added.

Saxon shook his head. "No, thank you," he said quietly. "I'll sit here for a while longer. Maggie!"

She turned from the doorway. "Yes, sir?"

He hesitated. "When you feel up to it, come back and talk to me."

"Yes, sir," she murmured.

They said the longest journey began with a single step. And that invitation was the first for Maggie. She was smiling when she followed her sister and Mrs. Tremayne up the staircase.

CHAPTER THREE

"It's going to be just lovely having some women in the house." Sandra Tremayne sighed as she lifted her coffee cup to her lips after the elegant china had been cleared from the table.

"Reverse chauvinism," Randy remarked, lifting the remainder of his wine in a mock toast.

"You don't know how lonely it is for me," the older woman accused.

"It wouldn't be so bad if Saxon would stop chasing nurses out into the night," Randy remarked dryly, with a glance at his somber stepbrother, who was sipping his coffee at the head of the table without, to Maggie's amazement, spilling a drop.

"I don't think Maggie would run," Saxon remarked with a faint smile. "Fate has a way of tossing her back to me when she tries, doesn't it, Maggie?" he added with cynical amusement.

Maggie picked at her crumpled linen napkin. There was a bite in his voice, and if she hadn't realized it, before, it was beginning to dawn on her that he hadn't forgotten his resentments, as he'd called them. They were simply tucked beneath the surface of his abrasive personality, ready to manifest themselves at a moment's notice.

"I came under my own power," she reminded him.

"And if you'd known who I was?" he demanded coolly, his eyes faintly cruel. "Would you still have come to see about the blind man?"

"Don't look to me for pity, you black-hearted beast," Maggie shot back. "You aren't helpless!"

He threw back his head and roared with laughter, while his stepmother and stepbrother stared, started, and began to smile. So that was how the lion had to be handled! And they'd been sympathetic, almost pandering to him.

"You hard-nosed little cat," Saxon chuckled. "I'll bet you bleed ink."

"Coffee," she corrected.

He leaned back in his chair with a sigh. "I know. I live on it too."

"You drink far too much of it, dear," Sandra noted. "It's a miracle your skin hasn't turned. I read about a man who drank and ate only carrot juice and carrots," she added. "He died, and his skin was orange. . . ."

"I'm not surprised," Randy laughed. "But, Mother, what about the time you went on that grapefruit diet? You didn't develop an acid personality."

"Cute, Randy." Lisa laughed.

"That's why you're marrying me, surely?" he returned.

"By the way, have you set a date?" Sandra asked seriously. "We have to decide on a gown for Lisa, and sent out invitations and arrange about the flowers. . . ."

"How about Christmas Eve?" Randy asked Lisa. "I've always wanted to be married then."

"It would have to be in the morning," Mrs. Tremayne reminded them, "because of the midnight service. We're Presbyterian, you know," she added.

"So are we," Lisa said, laughing. "How's that for a nice coincidence?"

"Lovely!" Sandra burst out, and smiled. "Oh, it will be the most beautiful wedding. Let me tell you what I think about flowers. Since it will be Christmas, we could—"

"Just a minute, Sandra," Saxon said, pushing his chair back from the table. "Maggie, let's go into the living room. Talking about weddings gives me indigestion."

"Yes, go ahead, dear," Sandra said, subdued, watching them leave the room, the big man allowing himself to be guided by the slender woman. There was something akin to pity in her eyes.

Maggie positioned Saxon in front of his big chair before the hearth and took the seat beside it as he eased down into the soft cushions.

"Well, you've charmed my family," he murmured when he'd lighted his cigarette and crossed his legs to get comfortable.

"It's mutual," she answered quietly. The flames were hypnotic; their heat cozy and pleasant. To sit there in that room with him was like coming home, Maggie thought. She didn't understand why, but she found pleasure in it.

He shifted restlessly, his eyes staring straight ahead. "I wish to God I could see you," he muttered. "Have you changed? Are you thinner, heavier? Is

43

your hair still long or have you had it cut? Come here!"

The whip in his voice startled her into movement. She stood up uncertainly.

"Here, in front of me," he growled, motioning her down between his knees, his big hands catching at her pant-clad legs to coax her.

His touch brought back memories. He'd only done that when necessary, to help her out of cars, or through doors, but his fingers had sent wild chills down her spine every time he'd put them on her, and she'd never got over it. Now, with the months of missing him adding to the excitement, her heart went wild when he leaned forward and cupped her face in his warm, strong hands.

"This is the only way I have of seeing you now," he said quietly. "Do you really mind?" he asked gently.

"No," she whispered. "No, I don't mind."

"Your voice is unsteady," he remarked. "Are you afraid I might choke you?"

"No, sir," she replied, closing her eyes as his thumbs ran over them, over her thin eyebrows and down over her long patrician nose to her soft bow-shaped mouth and then around the outline of her oval face with its high, elegant cheekbones. His fingers were just slightly callused, as if he'd been riding lately, and they felt deliciously abrasive on her whisper-soft skin as he touched it, finally running his hands over her short dark hair. He sighed heavily.

"You've had it cut," he murmured.

"I—it got in my way," she lied, knowing full well she'd had it cut because he'd once liked it.

"I remember how it looked that day we walked through the park," he said gently, his voice deep and slow in memory. "It was blowing out of control, and I got you a piece of ribbon from the flower vendor to tie it with."

"And a bouquet of violets to go with it," she added, hurting with the memory. It had been such a bittersweet day, the last she'd had with him before the story hit the stands.

His hands tightened on her face. "Let it grow again," he said gruffly.

"If you like." She looked up into his sightless eyes, and she wanted to cry. They were sensuous, with chips of gold in their tawny depths, with lashes any woman would have envied, and lines at the corners. The brows above them were thick and dark, and she wanted badly to reach up and touch them.

"I'm not through," he said quietly, his eyes seeming to searching her face as he held it in his big dark hands. "I want to know how you've changed physically, and this is the only way left to me. Will it offend you to let me touch you?"

Her eyes closed on a wave of pain. To feel his big hands touching her body was as close to heaven as she expected to come on earth. *Offend* her?

"No," she whispered unsteadily. "It won't . . . offend me."

He caught her by the shoulders and drew her to her feet as he rose, holding her in front of him. His fingers released her and began a journey of discovery that made her tremble with delight. They traced her arms through the silky Qiana blouse that was the same shade of dark green as her eyes, discovering

45

that they were as thin as ever. They ran back up to her shoulders and traced them to her long, elegant neck, then down to her collarbone.

"You're very thin," he said gently, pausing at the V neck of the blouse.

"I—I always lose weight a little in the autumn," she faltered.

"Do you?" His fingers moved again, down over the high, smooth slope of her breasts, and he felt her stiffen and jerk as they lingered on the beginning of the soft curves.

"I know, it's intimate," he said softly, scowling as his fingers traced tiny patterns through the fabric and the flimsy lace of the bra under it. "And you aren't used to letting a man touch you this way, are you?" Without waiting for an answer, he moved his hands completely over her high breasts, then down over her rib cage to her waist, her narrow hips, and finally to her thighs.

"You're so thin you tear at my heart," he said in a voice that puzzled her. "Did you eat supper?"

"Yes, sir," she told him.

"From now on see to it that you eat a big breakfast, and don't skimp on lunch. If I find out that you've been cutting meals, I'll feed you myself, is that clear?" he added shortly.

"Being thin is the rage right now," she said, defending herself, unwilling to admit that the reason for her slenderness was grieving over being away from him all this time.

"I don't want you thin," he replied. "I want you the way you were when I could still see. You had the loveliest figure I'd ever seen. High, firm breasts, a

46

small waist, and hips that were utterly tempting. I want you that way again."

She flushed at the speech. "Doesn't it matter that I might not want to gain weight?" she managed.

His hands slid back up to her waist and pulled her body close against his. "No," he replied honestly.

Her hands pressed patterns into his silky brown velour shirt, feeling the hard muscles under the softness of the fabric, warm from his big body. "Saxon . . ." she began nervously.

He bent. "I like the way you say my name," he whispered, his warm breath smoky against her lips. "Say it again."

This was getting too close for comfort, and she tried to make him let go. But he only held her tighter.

"Don't fight me," he murmured absently. "Pound for pound, I'm twice your size."

"Don't," she pleaded quietly, hating the sensations his careless caresses were causing. "You're just lonely, and you've been without a woman for a long time. . . ."

"What makes you think so?" he murmured with a mocking smile. "I may be blind, but that doesn't stop the wolf pack from stalking me. Didn't you know? Randy's been running interference for months—or I'd be shaking them out of my mattress. They think the sympathetic nurse approach will touch my cold heart."

"How amusing," she muttered, laughing involuntarily.

"That's something I'd never expect you to do," he added solemnly. "Money never mattered, did it? You'd have spent time with me if I'd had nothing—

47

as long as I was newsworthy," he added with sudden bitterness, and for an instant his hands were cruel were they gripped her.

"Saxon, I didn't betray you," she whispered, gritting her teeth against the bruising fingers. "I didn't!"

His mouth crushed down onto hers, finding it blindly, hurting as he took out the memories on her soft lips, twisting them so violently under his teeth that he cut them, and she cried out. It was like being tossed onto the rocks by storm-torn waves; he was brutal and tears welled in her eyes. She'd wanted him eight months ago with an almost shocking passion, and despite her nunlike upbringing, she'd have given herself to him joyfully in the throes of her growing love. But this was hardly worthy of her daydreaming; this was an experience that was more assault than ardor.

As if he sensed the tears, he lifted his dark head and scowled. His heart was thudding roughly against his chest, his breath came hard and fast.

"I'm hurting you?" he asked curtly.

She licked her cut lip and managed to catch her own breath. "Please let me go," she said through her tight throat.

His big hands relaxed their bruising grip and he murmured something gruffly under his breath. His blind eyes shifted restlessly.

"I tasted blood on your mouth," he said heavily. "Are you all right?"

She swallowed nervously. "It was . . . just a cut. I'm all right. Saxon, let me go, please!"

"I used to wonder how it would be to kiss that pretty mouth," he said softly. "I didn't mean it to be like this though. Don't struggle," he said, subduing her effortlessly. "Let me have your mouth one more time. Let me . . . make amends," he murmured, bending again.

This time his mouth was exquisitely gentle, rubbing against hers with a slight teasing pressure that was as tender as a baby's touch. His big arms swallowed her like warm bathwater, coaxing her body to relax, to allow the touch of his, to soften and melt into him.

"You taste like a virgin," he whispered into her mouth, twisting her body sensuously against the length of his, and his lips smiled tenderly against hers. "Are you?"

"Are you?" she returned with what spirit she could muster, her voice sounding as wobbly as her legs.

"Not for half my life," he replied. "Can't you tell?"

She could, but she wasn't going to admit it. Her fingers pushed against his chest. "Saxon—"

"Don't you want to unbutton my shirt, Maggie?" he whispered sensuously, nibbling tenderly at her full lower lip. "Haven't you wondered what it would be like to touch my skin?"

Her face flamed. Her blood surged up in her veins and ran in full flood. Yes, she'd wondered, and she wanted to, but giving in to Saxon now would be a step toward emotional suicide. He wasn't sure himself whether he wanted her, or just revenge, and she wasn't sure enough of him to find out.

She was debating on how to tell him all that when the door opened suddenly.

Maggie ducked under his arms and got around beside him just as Mrs. Tremayne, Lisa, and Randy walked in, talking and laughing and unaware of the undercurrents in the far end of the room.

CHAPTER FOUR

Blessedly nobody seemed to connect Maggie's red face and Saxon's smug smile, and the conversation became general. She sat on the sidelines, watching Lisa smiling comfortingly at her, and felt herself relax. Her lip, where Saxon had bitten it, no longer bothered her.

She studied the big imposing man in the big chair beside the fireplace with covetous eyes. He was so good to look at, so good to touch. Part of her was disappointed that the others had chosen that moment to interrupt, while another part felt relief. He wasn't sure himself whether he hated her or not, and while she might enjoy the touch of his hands, she couldn't take the harsh accusation in his voice without reacting to it. He'd frightened her, shocked her, by turning out to be the man who blamed her for his predicament. But Maggie was spirited, and she had a temper. And she wasn't going to let any man—even Saxon Tremayne—walk all over her.

A corner of her full mouth turned up. So he was determined to keep her here, was he? She'd let him think he was bulllying her into staying. He was right about one thing; he did, very definitely, need someone to keep him from tumbling headfirst into a long bout of self-pity. The man she remembered had been obsessively athletic, enjoying horseback riding, polo, tennis, and handball. He was an excellent swimmer as well, and he was always restless, eager to be up and away. When she'd been working on the disastrous feature, she'd had to follow him around just to get any information at all.

The man sitting so quietly in his chair now was a stranger. He still barked as the old Saxon Tremayne had. But some of that magnificent spirit was lacking; the bounding self-confidence was gone. Remembering the way he'd been, it hurt her to watch him. She shifted in her chair, her eyes worried. Somehow she'd have to help him cope, if she could. She'd have to make him go out of the house, meet other people, learn to stand by himself again. And she'd do that, she told herself. One way or another she was going to help him—even if he didn't want to be helped—and she didn't kid herself that it was going to be easy. He had a magnificent temper, one that matched his towering physique, and it was going to take cunning as well as kindness to get him back on his feet.

"You're very quiet, Miss Reporter," Saxon called suddenly, causing an immediate lull in the conversation about the nearby mountains and the blazing beauty of autumn in the upstate this month.

"Am I?" Maggie asked. "I was wondering if you'd like to take a drive up in the mountains one day."

His face hardened, his eyes kindled. "What for?" he asked curtly. "Do you expect my eyes to be miraculously restored?"

"You don't have to see to appreciate beauty," she

returned, watching him closely. "Of course, if you'd rather hide in here . . ."

"Hide?" he exploded, and his mother smothered a grin.

"Well, what would you call it?" Maggie asked reasonably. "You never leave the house, do you?"

He shifted angrily in the chair that just barely contained his formidable body. "I won't be led around like a half-witted child," he said proudly.

"You won't be," she promised. "You know, you really ought to be flattered. I don't offer my company to just anybody. And I certainly don't take men driving every day."

The teasing seemed to get through the armor around him. He pursed his chiseled lips and cocked an eyebrow. "How do I know you can hold a car in the road?"

"You don't," she agreed, and laughed. "You'll just have to trust me not to do you in. Besides, I'll be in the car too. I'll have to be careful."

He drew in a deep breath. "All right. In the morning if it isn't raining."

"What's wrong with rain? Do you melt if you get wet?" she asked him.

He lifted a bushy eyebrow. "Don't be smug, miss," he murmured with a glint in his sightless eyes. "I know very well what melts you, or don't you remember?"

She averted her red face. "You'll have to get Saxon to take you by the company while you're out," Sandra remarked, noting the color in Maggie's face and guessing the reason for it.

53

Saxon's face darkened, his big hands went taut on the arms of his chair. "That's out," he said firmly.

"But, dear," Sandra argued gently, "it would do you good—"

He got to his feet impatiently. "I'll decide what's good for me," he said curtly. "Where's that damned coffee table? I'm forever tripping over it. I can't understand why you people insist on moving it around!"

Maggie got to her feet, moved by Sandra's worried face. "Stop growling at people," she told Saxon, moving close to take his big hand gently in hers. For a moment she was sure he was going to shake it—and her—off. But after a brief hesitation his warm fingers curled around hers and pressed them possessively, sending a warm current through her body.

"Going to lead me around, are you?" he asked sharply.

She winked at the others. "No, sir," she said pertly. "I thought I'd let you lead me."

"Oh?" He smiled faintly. "What would you like to walk into first? A chair, a wall?"

"How about the front porch?" she suggested. "The sun's come out, and the mountains in the distance are glorious."

"I wouldn't know," he replied.

"I'll describe them to you," she offered, tugging at his hand. "Excuse us while we argue in peace," she told the others, who laughed softly as the two went out the door.

"Are we going to argue?" Saxon asked when she

seated him beside her in the glider on the long, grace-ful front porch.

She drank in the sweet, crisp autumn air, her eyes on the brightly colored leaves of the distant trees that covered the Blue Ridge Mountains. "It seems to be all you want to do," she replied.

"Like hell it is," he murmured, reaching out until he found her hand. He curled her fingers into his and leaned back with a hard sigh. "I've missed you."

"Have you?" She looked up at his hard face and something inside her melted. She wanted to admit just how much she'd missed him, but it might give him a weapon to beat her with, and she didn't know yet how far her trust of him would reach. His mood swings were too sudden.

He laughed curtly. "Don't believe me, do you? What's wrong, honey? Do you think I'm looking for weaknesses before I attack?"

"Aren't you?" she returned.

He shrugged his broad shoulders and released her hand to light a cigarette. He scowled as smoke curled up from the cigarette in his fingers. "I blamed you at first," he admitted. "My God, I've never hated any-one as much. I didn't expect that kind of betrayal from you. I thought we were close to the beginning of a very—different kind of relationship than the one we had."

Her eyes closed. She'd thought so too. The day before the issue had hit the stands carrying the story that had damned her in his eyes, there'd been one long moment when they'd stared at each other with all the camouflage removed; when his eyes and hers had echoed the same horrible hunger, the need that would almost certainly have been translated into fierce ardor if his office door hadn't been suddenly opened by a junior executive.

"Are you ever going to believe me?" she asked under her breath.

"I'm blind," he ground out, and took a vicious draw from his cigarette. "Have you any idea what it feels like to be without the sun, to live in shadow, to be totally dependent on other people? It's something that's never happened to me before, and I'm—" He stopped, chopping off the words abruptly to take another draw from the cigarette and blow it out. His heavy frame relaxed. "I'm not coping," he admitted finally. "Sometimes, at night, the pain is bad. I can't sleep, so I lie awake and brood. I can't run the company like this, not without eyes, so the whole burden falls on Randy, and he's not old enough or experienced enough to cope."

"What utter rot," she told him bluntly, turning in the seat to face him, warmed by the heat from his big body. "You can do anything a sighted man can do, if you'll just stop feeling sorry for yourself and try."

He stiffened, then exploded. "Feeling sorry for myself?" His face went rigid and his sightless eyes searched for her voice. "Damn you!"

It would have been less intimidating if he shouted, but that calm, cold voice had the cut of a sharp razor, and Maggie felt chills at the impact. But she wasn't going to back down, not one inch. Pity, despite the fact that she felt it, wouldn't help this proud, arrogant man to escape the prison he was making for himself. Only anger was going to do that.

"What would you call it, Mr. Tremayne?" she

taunted. "You sit in the house all day and refuse to help yourself. You won't go near your empire. What's the matter? Won't you be able to take it if somebody opens a door for you?"

The cigarette shot off the porch and he caught her shoulders in his big hands with amazing accuracy, shaking her roughly. "Stop it," he shot at her.

The feel of his hands made her weak-kneed, but not from fear. "Aren't you just afraid of pity, Saxon?" she whispered, watching his face as it came closer. "Isn't that what's wrong?"

His jaw clenched, his eyes narrowed, and she could see the arrow had hit home. His dark eyes closed and opened again. "Yes," he breathed.

Her hands found his face, tremulous hands, taking a liberty that once they wouldn't have dared. He flinched almost imperceptibly at the silken contact.

"How," she whispered, "could anyone pity a man like you? Don't you know that you're still more of a man, even without your sight, than most men are? Blind, lame, deaf, or paralyzed—you're still Saxon Tremayne. If you'll believe in yourself, you can do anything you want to. Anything."

She saw the flickering of indecision under his thick lashes. His hands where they gripped her upper arms had become gentle; holding, not hurting.

"I can't bear pity," he said.

"I'm glad," she replied, her voice lighter than she felt, "because I wouldn't presume to offer it to you."

"I won't use a damned cane," he warned.

She smiled through tears he couldn't see. "You'll have me, for a while. Then you can replace me with a Seeing Eye dog. Don't you like animals?"

57

"I don't know," he said quietly. "I've never had time for them."

"Dogs make nice pets," she said. "They're very intelligent, and they're softer than a cane. There are even new devices that can be surgically implanted to approximate sight."

"No," he said curtly.

"You could at least speak with a doctor. . . ."

"You could at least shut up," he murmured, and before she realized his intention, he bent forward and his mouth eased onto hers, his chiseled lips parting as they met hers, merging with them, opening them to the soft slow probing of his tongue.

Her hands on his cheeks hesitated for a second before they slid up into the thick silvered hair at his temples. Her own eyes closed, and her mouth yielded to his, wanting it, as the wind whipped softly around them, blending with the soft sounds of fabric sliding against fabric as he brought her closer.

It was heaven to be held like this, kissed like this. It had been so long, and she'd wanted him so during all the lonely months. She moaned softly at the force of the hunger. She'd never expected to feel such overpowering desire for a man; desire that made her ache in ways she never had, that made her legs tremble, her protests die before they ever reached the mouth he was devouring.

He drew back an inch, and his hand moved from her arm to the soft warm swell of her breast.

"No," she whispered, moving it up gently to her shoulder.

"I only want to 'see' what you look like," he murmured with a wicked smile.

"You already have," she reminded him.

"You've probably changed by now," he chuckled. "And I'm a poor blind man, without eyes to see."

"Pull the other one," she laughed. "You lecherous tycoon, you."

"I thought you were staying here to help me. My bed is quite large. . . ."

"Not that kind of help, and you very well know it," she returned.

His fingers traced up to find her lips, teasing the soft lines into a smile. His eyes sparkled with humor, the way they had so long ago when they could see her. "Are you still a virgin?"

She studied his face. "How do you know I was?"

"I didn't. But you weren't very worldly, Miss Sterline," he reminded her. "And it still bothers you to be touched with any intimacy. I'm just curious. I'd like to know if you've been with a man."

Her eyes found his collar, watching the heavy pulse that leaped against it. She sighed. "It isn't exactly in vogue these days, and most people don't believe me anyway—so I just let men think I'm being almighty selective and let it go at that."

"I take that to mean that you've never said yes?" he asked, his eyes more intent than she'd seen them so far.

She drew in a deep breath. "Yes," she admitted wearily. "I'm not trying to bring back the Victorian age," she added. "It's just that, for me, sex means commitment. Utter commitment to one man. And I've never found a man I cared to make a commitment to."

"You are a very attractive woman," he murmured,

reminiscence in his dark eyes as they stared blankly toward her. "Stacked, I believe the term is, and with a lovely face to match. There couldn't have been a shortage of offers."

"There hasn't been," she admitted. She smiled up at him; Maggie realized it was a smile he couldn't see, but it was in her voice all the same. "Yet," she added impishly.

He didn't smile. His fingers moved again, going over her delicate features lightly. "I want you," he said quietly, the words having all the more impact for their very softness. "I want the first time to happen with me."

Her breath caught in her throat. "Why?" she asked, drowning in his touch, in the soft words.

"Because some careless damned fool would hurt you. I wouldn't." His head went forward, his cheek drawing slowly, sensually, against hers, his breath warm at her ear. "I've never made love to a virgin," he whispered. "I've never wanted to until now. Do you know what a priceless thing you are?"

Her fingers contracted at the back of his head. She wanted to stretch like a cat, to feel her body move sinuously against his, and her own longings were faintly shocking. She could hardly breathe for the pounding of her heart.

"Is this part of it?" she managed, hating the words as she said them, but she was weakening, and she didn't dare. "Part of the scheme to make me pay for what you think I did?"

His body froze and tautened. He drew in a breath and moved away from her. All the old rigidity was back in his face; the tenderness had vanished from his cold brown eyes.

"You're sharp, aren't you?" he asked with narrowed eyes. "I'll have to be more careful from now on."

"You won't bring me to my knees, Mr. Tremayne," she said pertly, moving away from him. "But you're welcome to try."

"Don't you think I can, honey?" he asked, cocking an eyebrow. "This was just a minor skirmish. The battle is yet to come, and you're going to be here for a while."

"Only a couple of weeks," she replied firmly. "I do have a job that can't be held open indefinitely."

"We'll discuss that little problem some other time." He lighted another cigarette. "I thought we came out here to admire the view."

"So did I," she muttered, crossing her long legs. "What would you like to do about it? I could gather some leaves and toss them over you, along with a few pebbles, to give you the feel of the season."

"I could pitch you off this damned porch too," he chuckled. "Blind or not, it wouldn't take much effort."

She laughed with him, some of the tension gone. Her eyes drifted out toward the highway to the backdrop of blue mountains.

"How long have your people lived here?" she asked.

"In Jarrettsville?" he asked. "Oh, a hundred and fifty years or so. The Jarrett who founded the town was an ancestor."

"And your stepmother's family?" she asked.

61

He grinned. "Carpetbaggers." He chuckled. "I dearly love to tease her about it. Sandra's the salt of the earth; she can take a joke—even at her expense—and don't think she doesn't give it back. She isn't a fiery woman, but she's damned stubborn. Her people were Steeles from Chicago. Her grandfather settled here and went into the textile business, just as my people had. It's a major industry in this part of the state."

"And you had your biggest branch in Charleston," she recalled. "Not here."

He smiled. "My mother's people were from Charleston," he told her. "As a matter of fact, my grandfather's father—my great-grandfather—was town marshal there for a while until he was killed trying to arrest a man. I still have the old pocket watch he carried, with his initials carved inside the back. It's quite a treasure."

"I guess so," she agreed. She smiled and sighed. "I have a few treasures from my mother's side of the family. An old Confederate pistol, and some crystal and silver. Not very much, I'm afraid; my people weren't wealthy."

"Neither were mine, honey, not at first. They came over here from Scotland with the clothes on their backs, and a lot of determination to make some kind of better life for themselves."

"They seem to have done that," she commented.

"Not without some effort. It still takes a lot of effort to coordinate the plants and keep them going." He began to brood again, and she punched him in the arm playfully.

"All the more reason to get you back on your

feet," she said with a laugh. "Now, how would you like me to walk you around the yard a few times and teach you how not to trip over the roots of the oak trees?"

His head tilted back. "It would be like you to lead me right into the damned tree."

"Who me?" she asked innocently.

"Yes, you, Snow White," he returned. "But you'd better keep one thing in mind before you trip me up."

"What's that?" she asked, rising with him.

"If I fall, I'll fall on you."

She stared at his bulk and sighed with theatrical perfection. "Oh, my, I'd better make sure you don't," she told him. "I'd be a little flat bit of color on the ground, wouldn't I?"

"If we fall," he murmured, bending down, "I'll have other things on my mind than leaving you flat."

"Well, I won't ask what," she promised, taking his hand. "I'm a good girl, I am, and I'm not letting any lecherous tycoon lead *me* astray!"

He laughed as she helped him walk down the steps. It was a beginning at least.

CHAPTER FIVE

Later in the upstairs bedroom that Maggie had been given for the length of her stay, she and Lisa sat talking after they'd dressed for dinner.

"I thought you were a goner," Lisa said with a laugh, glancing at her older sister, who was wearing an emerald-green chiffon dress that matched her eyes.

"You weren't the only one," Maggie confessed. "I don't think I've ever had such a shock that I couldn't even fight back. When Randy mentioned that his older brother was Saxon Tremayne, I was sure my life was over."

"He's a dish, isn't he?" Lisa murmured unexpectedly, her eyes calculating.

"Who? Randy?" came the dry reply.

"You know very well I meant Saxon," Lisa said, pursing her lips.

Maggie's eyes fell to the floor, to the white shag carpet that set off the royal-blue velvet bedspread on the four-poster and the heavy matching curtains at the windows. "I thought he hated me. I'm still not sure that he doesn't. All this talk about helping him get his bearings might just be a cover-up, something to keep me here while he plots revenge."

"If the way he was clinging to your hand was any indication, I wish Randy hated me that way."

Maggie smiled. "He was making sure that if I ran him into a wall, I'd go too. What am I going to do about my job? You know they'll never be able to go two weeks without me."

"Everybody is expendable," her sister reminded her. "They'd have to do without you if you died. Besides, I have a feeling that Mr. Tremayne has already taken care of it."

She winced. "I never dreamed that it would be like this for him," she murmured, her green eyes troubled. "Lisa, what if it was my fault? What if his sight never comes back?"

Lisa touched her arm gently. "Stop that. All you have to do is concentrate on helping him get his confidence back. And if you care as much as I think you do, that shouldn't be very hard for you, should it?"

Maggie stood up with a sigh. "I know what I feel," she confessed. "It's what *he* feels that's going to keep me up nights. I won't worry about it right now though. We'll go down and have supper, and then I'll try to live one day at a time."

"A very practical solution, if you ask me," came the amused reply.

But Maggie didn't feel practical. She felt confused, hungry, and frightened. Sitting next to Saxon at the long table under the crystal chandelier, she had a crazy impulse to get up and run.

He was as sensuous a man as any woman could

ever have wanted, she thought, watching his beige silk shirt strain across his massive chest under the tweed jacket. The thick, dark shadow of hair-roughened muscles was just visible through the thin fabric. Maggie had never seen Saxon without a shirt, but she was suddenly aware that she wanted to. She wanted to touch him. . . .

Shocked by the force of her own longing, she dug into her food with a vengeance, keeping hidden the eyes that he couldn't see.

"You're very quiet, Maggie," he murmured gently.

She glanced up nervously and smiled, forgetting for an instant that he couldn't see her. "I'm just busy concentrating on this delicious food," she lied, adding silently, *which could be cardboard for all my taste buds are telling me.*

He cocked his shaggy head to one side, his dark eyes faintly amused. "Are you sure?"

"What do you think is the matter with me then?" she asked, taking the argument into his own camp. "That I'm sitting here mooning over you?"

He threw back his dark head and laughed, and Sandra and Randy stared at him, amazed. Apparently laughter was a rare commodity in the big dark man since his accident.

"Are you?" he asked. "Mooning, I mean?"

"If you must know," she muttered, "I'm worrying about what I'll do if you suddenly take a notion to drive when we go out in the morning."

That brought laughter from the other members of the family as well and effectively ended his pointed questioning.

66

The next morning Maggie donned a pleated green plaid skirt and a green sweater with her bone-colored boots before she went downstairs. She felt a strange new excitement at the thought of being totally alone with Saxon, having him all to herself even for a few hours. It was something she'd dreamed about before the story broke and ruined things between them.

Saxon was already at the breakfast table, but the others were nowhere in sight.

"Maggie?" he asked softly, lifting his head when he heard her soft footsteps, and something in his tone made her blood run wild.

"Yes," she replied, seating herself next to him at the long table. "I thought you said to get down here by seven."

"I did."

"But where are the others?" she persisted.

"Still in bed," he murmured with a faint smile. "No need to rouse the whole household just because we're going out, is there?"

"No, of course not." She had to tear her eyes away from him. He was wearing a white turtleneck sweater under the same beige tweed jacket he'd been wearing the night before, with tan slacks, and Maggie thought he looked good enough to eat. "Would you like some more coffee?" she asked, lifting the pot.

"I haven't had any yet," he replied. "I was waiting for you."

She smiled secretly. "Should I be flattered?"

"That would depend on how hungry I was," he replied, "and I'm keeping that bit of information to myself. How about putting some eggs on my plate, honey? I sent Mrs. Simpson out to get the mail from our post office box."

She obliged him, reaching for the platter of bacon and country ham when she'd put the eggs down. "Bacon or ham?" she asked.

"Bacon, but try the ham yourself," he told her. "It came from the farm."

She studied him. The house was sitting on a lot of land, and she'd noticed the white-fenced pastures around it with curiosity. "Is this a farm?" she asked.

He grinned. "Very astute, Miss Sterline. Yes, it is a farm, and we raise most of our own meats and vegetables."

She sighed. He was apparently more of an out-doorsman than she'd even guessed. That would make his blindness an added burden. She added a huge, fluffy cat's-head biscuit to his plate and her own.

"Butter?" she asked.

"Please."

She buttered both biscuits quickly and told him where everything was on his plate, using the numbers of a clock as indication points. Surprisingly he didn't make any snide comments about her directions as he began to eat—and without losing a single morsel.

"You've gone quiet again," he mentioned after a minute.

"I was thinking that you must have enjoyed working around the farm . . . before," she confessed.

His dark face clouded, and she could have bitten her tongue for the hasty remark. "Yes," he said curtly. "I did a lot of riding as well."

She looked up. "You could still ride, couldn't you?" she asked.

"With a companion, I suppose so," he said non-committally. "Do you ride, Maggie?"

"A little." She grinned. "I fall off if I have to go very fast, though."

That seemed to restore a little of his lost humor. "You could ride with me," he suggested. "I could hold you on, and you could point me in the right direction."

She looked at him. Just the thought of being so close to him took her breath away. She could almost feel the warmth, the powerful muscles, against her. "Sure," she countered. "And if you fell off, you'd take me with you and crush me!"

He looked toward the sound of her voice, his hard face with its strong lines sensual, like his voice when he spoke. "I'd like very much to crush you," he murmured. "Under me. All of you."

She felt the blush that ran into her cheeks and lifted the coffee cup to her lips. She wouldn't have touched that line with a ten-foot pole.

"Won't play?" he murmured with a wicked smile. "We'll see about that. Finish your breakfast, honey. We've got a lot of ground to cover today."

She leaned forward. "Where are we going—besides for a ride?"

"To my office," he said with a rough sigh.

She smiled secretly. That would be the biggest step he'd taken since the accident, and she couldn't help feeling proud that she'd had a part in it. She lifted her fork and stabbed a piece of country ham from its platter.

When they finished breakfast, she held his arm,

half guiding him out to the garage where the family cars were kept.

Inside were a Mercedes, a Fiat, and a big black Lincoln town car.

"Which one is yours?" she asked uncertainly.

"Guess."

She studied his lofty face. "The Lincoln."

He cocked an eyebrow and smiled. "Should I be flattered that you know my taste?"

She laughed. "I don't know."

His arm reached around her shoulders, holding her close to his side. "I need a big car, honey. There's a lot of me to squeeze in it."

She nudged him playfully. "I'll vouch for that," she agreed, tugging him toward the car. "Well, I just hope I won't rip off the fenders getting us out of here. I drive a Volkswagen, you know."

"My God," he said, laughing. "You *are* going to have some adjusting to do. I'll trust you, though, Maggie. With the car at least," he added in an undertone that bothered her.

He paused as she was trying to put him in the passenger side. "Just a minute." His hands ran from her shoulders down to her waist, making her tremble with the unexpectedly sensual exploration. "What are you wearing? Describe it to me."

She did, her voice straining from the sudden contact with his big hands as he held her; Maggie realized their bodies were almost touching.

"What kind of sweater is it?" he murmured, and reaching up, traced the V neckline with one long, probing finger. "Soft skin," he murmured gently.

The exploring finger eased inside the neckline to trace the slope of her breast. "Very, very soft."

She caught his trespassing fingers and held them in her own. "Shame on you," she told him.

He only laughed. "Are you blushing? I'm sorry I can't see you, Maggie, I have a feeling your eyes are giving away the whole show." His face clouded suddenly, and he let go of her with a sigh. "We'd better get on the road."

She moved away from him, feeling both relief and disappointment. If only she could trust him not to hurt her. But she still didn't know if revenge was motivating him, and until she found out, she didn't dare let him get too close.

CHAPTER SIX

This part of western South Carolina was largely foot-hills leading to the majestic Blue Ridge Mountains. Now, with autumn painting them in carnival colors, the view was so breathtaking that his blindness seemed faintly obscene.

"It's cool out today," Saxon remarked, his sightless eyes facing forward while Maggie drove the big car down the highway.

"Yes, it is. I only wish you could see the mountains," she remarked gently. "They look as if some overeager artist has taken a palette of gold and red and orange and amber and flung each color at them with the tip of his brush."

One corner of his wide mouth curved. "You do that very well—the description. Where are we?"

She named the highway. "It's very long, and there isn't much traffic right now. The mountains are ahead of us in the distance and we're driving through what used to be hills. There's love grass curling down the banks."

"Love grass?" he asked with a cocked eyebrow.

"Truly," she laughed, "that's what it's called. Our soil conservation people in Georgia plant it to keep down erosion on high banks, just as they put rock rip-rap on stream beds to keep the banks from washing away. I suppose your own soil conservation people are responsible for doing it here."

"We ought to be near Jarrettsville now," he remarked, changing the subject as he shifted in his seat.

"Just over the hill," she agreed, watching the small city come into view against the colorful backdrop of the mountains. "It's bigger than I remembered," she murmured. "But just as lovely."

"I've always thought so," he said. "It's not as big as Anderson or Spartanburg or Greenville, but it's still a formidable textile center."

"Your corporation is the most formidable member, I recall," she said with a smile.

"We started out small," he told her. "But we're still growing, despite the economy. Where are we?"

She told him. "As I remember, we turn right here," she said.

"Yes, and then left."

"But does that go behind the plant?"

"It goes to the computer center," he said. "Where my main office is. You've never been there."

She followed his directions in silence, recalling that period in her life that had ended in such tragedy. She remembered several visits to the gigantic Tremayne Corporation's mills, but somehow the computer center had never been on the agenda. At the time she and Saxon had been concerned mainly with the production end of the business. He'd mentioned the place where the corporation's nerve center was located, but she'd never really been that interested. She'd been far more interested in the man himself,

73

and his publicity department had provided her with all the photos of the operation that she'd required for her disastrous story.

She parked the car near the entrance to the computer center and cut off the ignition. But when she started to get out, he was sitting rigidly in his seat, staring straight ahead with a scowl above his sightless eyes.

"Coming in?" she asked gently.

He drew in a deep, impatient breath. "I don't know if this is a good idea."

"Why not?" She eyed him mischievously. "Afraid of swooning female employees tripping over you?"

He looked startled for an instant, and then laughter burst out of him and washed away the taut lines in his broad face. "God, you're good for my ego," he chuckled.

"Anytime," she told him. "Now, shall we get out, or would you rather sit here and brood for the rest of the morning? Just think how suspicious it would look if any of your executives happened to see us sitting here."

"Oh, I don't think it would look suspicious," he murmured, and before she realized what he was planning, he reached out and caught her, jerking her across the seat and onto his lap.

"Saxon. . . ." she breathed jerkily.

His face was somber, unreadable, as his warm fingers Brailled her face, lingering on the soft curve of her mouth. "Nervous?" he murmured. "There's no need. What could I do to you here?"

"Would you like a list?" she asked. "We'd better go in, hadn't we?"

74

"I don't want to go in yet," he replied. His fingers tilted her chin so that she could feel his warm, smoky breath against her lips. "I could eat you!" he breathed, bending.

She felt the hard crush of his mouth with a wild aching in the most improbable places. She didn't even try to fight. The feel of him was too exciting, like an aged wine that she craved. Her body lifted into his arms as if it was the most natural thing in the world. She'd never cared so much about another human being—not even members of her family. He was the light of her whole existence, and denying him was impossible for her. Blind or not, he was still Saxon.

Her mouth gave him back the kiss. Her arms reached around his neck, and she clung to him. She could hear the hard sigh of his breath, feel the rough hunger in his big body as he pressed her hips into his with a grinding motion.

"Oh!" She gasped into his mouth at the unaccustomed intimacy.

He heard the tiny sound and smiled against her lips. His hand pressed harder at the base of her spine, and he lifted his head, alert to the tiniest sound, the smallest movement.

"Why, Maggie, did you think blindness had made me impotent?" he asked outrageously.

She struggled up and away from him, aware all the time that she'd never have got away unless he'd wanted her to. He sat there, delighted with himself, and she glared at him from a face frankly red with embarrassment while he laughed softly.

"Will you hush?" she grumbled as she struggled to

75

restore some kind of order to her appearance in the rearview mirror, uncomfortably aware of the lingering desire in his broad face that matched the desire she'd felt for the first time.

"I can't help it. I'm not used to dealing with nervous virgins. It's . . . intoxicating."

"I'm not nervous," she denied shortly.

"You're definitely unsophisticated," he returned softly. "You make my head swim with the possibilities."

"Just you forget about the possibilities and concentrate on being a successful businessman, will you?" she muttered.

"I think I'd rather be your lover, Maggie," he returned in a tone that made her knees wobbly.

"Can we go?" Was that tiny squeak really her voice? she asked herself.

He grinned. "If you're afraid to pursue this very interesting conversation, I suppose we can postpone it until later."

"That's what you think," she mumbled as she got out of the car and went around to guide him toward the building.

The Tremayne Corporation's main office sat on several acres of beautifully landscaped grounds and easily filled two tremendous buildings and two smaller ones. Maggie remembered the biggest as being the main mill, where fibers became fabric. The other large building was the sewing plant, where garments were made and finished. The two smaller buildings were the distribution center and the computer center.

She noticed the Tremayne Corporation logo on

the computer center, with its distinctive oversize red *T,* and smiled. It suited Saxon, that bold color. If he'd been a color, he'd have been red, because he was so vivid.

His fingers tightened on hers as they went up the few steps and into the modern building. The lobby was filled with potted trees and plants, making it spacious and welcoming.

"I like this," she murmured as they walked toward the redheaded receptionist. "It's like an Oriental garden, complete with miniature waterfall," she added, noting the lush vegetation surrounding the small artificial waterfall against one wall.

"I had it designed that way," he said curtly. "The girl at the desk—is she about your age and a flaming redhead?"

"Yes," she agreed, watching amusedly the look of surprise on the redhead's face when she caught sight of the big dark man and his companion.

"Mr. Tremayne!" the secretary exclaimed, rising, her face smiling and excited. She rushed from behind the desk with an apologetic glance at Maggie and grinned at Saxon. "Well, it's about time you made an appearance," she teased. "All this work piling up, and Randy carrying it off and losing half of it. . . ."

Saxon chuckled softly, visibly relaxing. "He'd damned well better not lose any of it. How are you, Tabby?" he asked.

"Well, it's pretty dull around here without you," she sighed, winking at Maggie, who smiled back. "So peaceful. No shouting, no cursing. . . ."

"It may not last long," he told her. "I want to

know what's been going on. Randy's hardly forth-coming, and to be truthful I've had my mind on other things."

"I'd hate being called an other thing," Tabby told Maggie. "I'm Octavia Blake—Tabby to my friends."

"Maggie Sterline," she replied, shaking hands. She liked the tall redhead already. "Which way do we go?"

"I'll show you. Coffee, boss?" she asked Saxon.

He nodded. "Black and strong, and put some cream in Maggie's."

"Will do," Tabby said, while Maggie caught her breath at his phenomenal memory. All these months, and he even remembered how she took her coffee!

Tabby left them in a huge immaculate office with a massive oak desk, leather furniture, and what looked like a microcomputer on a table beside the desk.

Maggie helped Saxon to the chair, and when he sat down behind it, it was like old times. The first time she'd ever seen him was behind a desk—at the sewing plant one building over. He'd been visiting his plant manager when she came in to ask about doing the feature story. And afterward they always seemed to meet in one plant or the other, or in town. She'd never seen this particular office.

"It suits you," she said, watching him lean back in the swivel chair.

"What does?" he asked.

"This office. It's solid and dependable and a little overpowering."

He laughed. "I feel a little overpowered myself right now." He clasped his hands behind his head, and the shirt strained sensuously against the hard muscles of his chest. "I used to take my sight so much for granted," he murmured. "Can you imagine how it feels to sit here, in this chair, with the responsibility that goes with it—and be blind?" His face hardened; his eyes glittered.

She closed her eyes on a wave of pain. "You'll cope with it," she told him firmly. "You'll manage."

"Manage," he scoffed. "If it hadn't been for that damned article of yours, I wouldn't have to manage!"

"And if you hadn't been speeding . . ." she began hotly, but before she could get out the words, Tabby came in with a tray, stopping her in midsentence.

"Here you are," Tabby said, smiling, oblivious to the dark undercurrents. "I filched a few doughnuts from the cabinet to go with them. I don't imagine you ate much breakfast—as usual," she said to Saxon.

"Efficient as always, Tabby. Maggie, will you amuse yourself for a few minutes while we talk business?" he added curtly, taking his coffee from Tabby after Maggie had picked hers up. "Turn on the computer, honey," he told his secretary, "and put in the file on the Bilings account. Randy said there was a problem."

"Problem isn't the word," Tabby murmured, taking out a floppy disk from its container. She turned on the computer, waited for the load signal, and slid the disk into its slot with a flick of her finger.

"Here you are," she said. "The biggest obstacle is their union. The workers are concerned about their jobs, and there's some crazy rumor that you're going to replace the older workers immediately so you won't have to pay retirement benefits. Isn't that incredible? The union is fighting the merger tooth and nail, threatening a walkout as soon as the papers are signed."

"Oh, hell," he said curtly. "It isn't the union, it's that vice-president of Bilings's—he wants the presidency of the company, and he's stirring up trouble deliberately to blackmail me into putting him in the executive chair. If he's promoted, no strike—he laughs off the rumor to the union, assures them that the older workers will be retained if he's made president, and uses that against me." His face darkened, but his eyes sparkled with challenge. "There's only one thing he hasn't counted on. I don't like blackmail. I'll go down there myself tomorrow and call a meeting with the union on the spot, and I'll make damned sure the plant's vice-president is there to hear every word."

"Going to fire him?" Tabby grinned.

"That's too easy," he replied, leaning back to sip his coffee. "I'm going to demote him to the ordering department and make his life hell for a few weeks. If he sticks it, I may give him the presidency. Read me the résumé on him."

Maggie, angry and frustrated at having to hold it all in, took her coffee and wandered around the room while Tabby read the file to her boss. There were photographs all around the room, showing every phase of the vertical mill operation from fiber to finished goods. Maggie recognized each phase of the operation from selection of fibers through carding, combing, the forming of the sliver (which, she remembered, rhymed with *diver*), drawing, and roving. It was fascinating to watch the fibers—either cotton, nylon, or polyester or blends of each—formed into the sliver, the loose rope made from the fibers, and then to watch the slow narrowing of the sliver through each process until it became yarn or thread. The sewing plant held as much fascination. It reminded Maggie of puzzle pieces: Each seamstress was responsible for a different operation as garments were slowly assembled from pieces cut in the cutting room to finished garments inspected by quality-control people.

Other photographs showed early days at the cotton mill, with wagons full of just picked cotton being unloaded in bales.

Finally, when she'd looked at each one twice, and Tabby was still reading, Maggie paused by the window, which faced the mountains. But she wasn't looking at the autumn splendor. Her mind was still on Saxon's unfounded accusation. She wanted to hurt him, as he'd hurt her.

She wasn't even aware that Tabby had finished speaking, or that Saxon had been barking out orders in his deep quiet voice, until he called her.

"Maggie, have you gone deaf?" he growled.

She jerked at the sound, turning. "There are times when it's better not to hear," she returned pointedly, joining him at the desk. "Are you ready to go?"

He tilted his head, aware of the bite in her tone. "What is it?" he asked.

Tabby murmured something and left them alone, closing the door behind her.

"Well?" Saxon persisted. He stood up, one big hand resting on the desk. "Maggie?"

She glared at him. "I've told you until I'm blue in the face that I didn't write that article," she said harshly. "What do I have to do to convince you?"

His face relaxed, but only a little. "Come here."

"We need to go—"

"For God's sake will you come here?" he ground out. "Maggie, don't make me stumble all over the room trying to find you!"

She hesitated, but only for an instant. She didn't really want to humiliate him. She moved forward.

He seemed to feel the heat of her body before she ever got to him, because he reached out and caught her shoulders, pulling her against him.

"I told you at the beginning that I tend to get impatient and short-tempered," he said quietly. "It won't get better, especially when the headaches come, so if you want to back out of the agreement and go home, I won't stop you."

The statement shocked her. It didn't sound like a man after revenge. She stared up into the unseeing dark eyes with her heart in her own—and all her resentments fell away. It wasn't fair, she thought bitterly, that he could undermine her resistance this way, just by being humble. And it was so obviously a false impression, because when had Saxon Tremayne ever been humble?

She sighed. "I've got a temper of my own, and I lose it far too often," she murmured. "Shouldn't we go?"

He drew her forehead against his chest with a sigh,

holding her gently, rocking her in his warm arms with his cheek against her dark hair. "Bear with me," he whispered at her ear. "I'm doing my damnedest not to hurt you."

It was quite a confession for the rigid, uncompromising man she remembered. She had a feeling that he never apologized.

"Said the wolf to the lamb," she laughed.

"You've got teeth yourself," he reminded her with a laugh. His arms tightened for an instant before he released her. "You wouldn't last long around me if you were one of those meek little angels most mothers want their daughters to grow into. Let's go home, honey. I've got to rout Randy out and talk tactics with him."

"You're the boss," she said, taking his hand to walk him out the door.

Tabby met them in the outer office. "Want me to pack up some of these little nagging problems and let you carry them off, boss?" she asked tongue in cheek.

"What kind of little nagging problems?" he asked.

"Well, for example," she rattled off, "there's the soft drink machine that masquerades as a one-armed bandit. There's the coffee machine that gives coffee but no cups. There's the computer repairman who promised to be here Monday and hadn't shown up Friday. There's the dogged apparel fastener salesman who wouldn't listen when I tried to tell him we were contracted to another supplier. There are the three girls who can't sew but want to start at twice the salary we pay production workers. . . ."

"Get me the hell out of here," Saxon told Maggie

with a loud laugh. "Take care of it, Tabby," he called over his shoulder.

The redhead stuck out her tongue as they left the building.

CHAPTER SEVEN

"Where to now?" Maggie asked when they were back in the car.

"That's up to you, honey. You're driving," he said with a smile.

"Want to ride up in the mountains and have a picnic?" she suggested, feeling elated and adventurous. "We could stop and get some cheese and crackers and cookies."

"Childhood revisited?" he chided.

"Something like that," she admitted. "Lisa and I used to go fishing with Dad, and we'd always stop at some little country store to get something to snack on. I'd all but forgotten what fun it was."

"I haven't been fishing since I was twelve," he recalled.

"What do you do for relaxation when you're not working yourself to death?" she asked after she'd cranked the car and pulled out onto the highway.

"The corporation has been my vocation and my avocation for years, Maggie," he said quietly. His hands dug for a cigarette and he lighted it with careless ease. "I haven't had time for anything else."

"It sounds rather narrow," she observed.

"Does it? What do you do when you're not working on the newspaper?"

She sighed. "Not a lot," she confessed. "We only have two reporters, and the other one is just part-time, after school. I'm on call twenty-four hours a day. If anything happens, I'm expected to cover it, regardless of what time it is."

"That doesn't sound very safe," he remarked. "What if there's a night robbery?"

"I get my camera and go," she said simply. "It's part of the job. News doesn't take holidays."

"Blind dedication," he scoffed.

"We're the public's eyes and ears," she argued, warming to battle. "We're writing history as it happens. Who's going to record important events for posterity if we don't?"

"I fail to see what difference it's going to make if a small-town bank robbery is recorded for posterity," he said shortly. "And does it really matter if you get the facts at midnight or at seven the next morning?"

She drew in a sharp breath. "You just don't understand."

"I never did. You give a hundred and ten percent to the job, and who cares? Not the people who read the stories. They knew everything before the paper went to press. They just read it to find out who got caught."

"You're oversimplifying."

"No, I'm not. You're overstating the importance of what you do. I've noticed that about dedicated journalists," he continued. "They see the job as a holy grail. It's nothing more than an overglorified gossip column, which sometimes causes more problems than it solves. I've seen radical groups parading for the benefit of television cameras."

"We do a lot of good," she muttered, executing a turn.

"Name something," he challenged.

"All right, I will." And she proceeded to rattle off projects the paper had supported—programs to benefit the needy, the homeless, the aged, the under-privileged, the uneducated, the bereaved, the blind, the victimized, the multiple-handicapped—and only when she paused for breath did he stop her with an upraised hand and an amused laugh.

"Okay, I get the picture," he admitted. "Maybe small-town papers accomplish more, and I won't argue that you do some good. But," he added, "will the world end if you give it up?"

She thought about that. "Not for the subscribers," she confessed. "Because there's always somebody who can replace you on a newspaper staff, and prob-ably do a better job than you did yourself. But I don't know if I could live without it, you see."

"Why not?" His head lifted, as if her answer seemed to matter intensely to him.

"It's not a dull job, and it's never routine," she replied. "There's always something going on, either a project you're following, or a big story beginning to break under wraps. You can't get bored, because you don't have the time." Her face lit up with the memories. "You get to go in the front door of places you couldn't get in the back door of if you were just an average citizen. You get to meet extraordinary people, do exciting things. I love it," she concluded. "It's . . . everything."

"A man should be that, to a woman," he said quietly.

"No man is ever going to be everything to me," she replied, easing the car onto the highway that led to the distant mountains.

"I wouldn't be overconfident if I were you," he advised. "Very often, none of us are as self-sufficient as we convince ourselves we are."

"Speaking from personal experience?" she challenged.

"Yes," he admitted, surprising her. "I never thought I'd live to see the day when I'd have to be led around by the hand like a child, Maggie. I'd have bet money that it could never happen."

"It won't always be like this for you," she told him with more conviction than she felt.

"Won't it?" he laughed bitterly. "That's not what my surgeon told me."

"Circumstances may change," she reminded him.

"Whales may drive cars some day," he retorted.

"Saxon . . ."

"Leave it, honey. Tell me where we are."

He wasn't going to discuss it any more, that was obvious. She sighed wearily. "We're heading out of Jarrettsville going west, and there's a highway leading off to our left across the Tyger River. Which way do I go?"

"Straight ahead. We should be in the foothills of the Blue Ridge Mountain chain by now."

"We certainly are," she laughed, noticing the hilly countryside, the open country, and the occasional cabin nestled among the glorious foliage.

He named two highways and added, "Where they

intersect, take the left fork and about three to four miles along, there'll be a small country store on the right. We can stop there and get some snacks."

"You've got a good memory," she remarked.

"I do my best. Are you familiar with mountain driving?"

"Not as used to it as I'd like to be," she admitted, "but I won't panic if the brakes get hot and start squealing. I've driven in the Georgia mountains up around Blairsville and Hiawassee. And believe me, that's good training!"

"I know what you mean. The curves are quite a challenge." His face hardened, and she knew he was remembering his racing days.

"Would you like to hear the news?" she asked, and before he could refuse, she turned on the radio, grateful for the small diversion that might keep him from brooding.

Minutes later they were climbing around some hairpin curves, and she wasn't nervous at all with Saxon beside her. Oddly enough he made her feel secure. She'd stopped at the little country store and stocked up with canned sausages, crackers, cookies, and soft drinks and some old-fashioned hoop cheese.

"It's beautiful here," she said, stopping at a deserted roadside park that overlooked the mountains.

"Deserted?" he asked.

"Oh, very. Shall we unload and stay awhile?"

"Suits me."

She helped him out of the car and, ignoring the cement tables and benches, they sprawled under a spreading maple tree, finishing off the cheese and crackers and sausages before they relaxed with soft drinks and cookies.

"It's so beautiful here," she said with a sigh, stretching back to close her eyes. "Cool and sweet-smelling and so peaceful."

"You're years too young to need peace," he observed.

"We all need it at times," she returned.

"Remind me to have a wheelchair brought in for you, Granny." He laughed, finishing off his soft drink. He lay back on the crisp leaves beside her with a sigh. "God, I needed this. The silence, the mountains, you. . . ."

She rolled over on her side to study him. Close up like this, he was a different man from the high-powered tycoon she'd glimpsed in his office earlier.

"A loaf of bread, a jug of wine . . ." she grinned.

"And thou," he murmured. He reached out to find her arm, and his fingers stroked it gently, sending little darts of sensation through her. "Come here, Maggie," he said softly.

"It's public," she hesitated.

"I'll hear a car before you will," he said quietly. His fingers tightened. "I—I need it, can you understand that? I need to prove to myself that I'm not half a man as well as a blind one. . . ."

What an unfair argument that was, she thought miserably, going to him without reservation. But it was out of love, not pity—something he couldn't know. The feel of his long hard body against hers was a foretaste of heaven, and all she wanted out of life at that moment.

"I've wanted this all day," he murmured, nuzzling

his mouth against her soft face until he searched out her warm lips. His hands pressed her toward him; the scent of him filled her nostrils. "I've wanted the taste of you, the feel of you against me—things I haven't had a lot of since you came back."

Her eyes closed, and she forced herself to relax, to yield to his strength. "You're very strong," she murmured, letting her hands trace his broad shoulders.

"And you're very soft," he replied. His hands moved up her rib cage to savor the high full curves of her breasts. "Especially here. . . ."

She started to protest, but his mouth was working magic on hers, as expert as she remembered, and just as dangerous as it mocked her faint protest at the intimacy of his fingers.

"Don't fight me," he murmured against her lips. "I'll confine my attentions to this very interesting territory, if that's what you want. Where are the buttons?"

She tried to concentrate, but he was stroking her lips with his tongue and her mind was somewhere in limbo, not on the unusual pattern of the buttons that were located under her arm.

"So," he murmured, finding them, and his fingers went to work, easing them apart. "And this little wisp," he whispered, unhooking the fastening of the bra that was little more than decoration. "Ah," he breathed as his hands found sweet, living warmth and felt her sudden stiffening, heard her wild gasp. "Maggie, you're like silk to touch," he breathed, "and so sweet that I could eat you!" He brought his mouth down against the taut, swelling rise of her body and savored the lightly scented skin with something rivaling reverence. "You taste of flowers," he whispered as she arched and bit her lip to keep from crying out, letting his hands lift her up to his gentle, searching mouth. He tasted her, nibbled at her, until a sharp cry burst from her lips with the force of the pleasure he was giving her.

"Maggie," he moaned softly, and moved his hands back down to cup her, stroke her. His mouth slid up to hers and took it roughly. His fingers contracted suddenly, and she cried out.

He stiffened, lifting his head, his hands quickly easing their rough grip. "I'm sorry," he said gently, "that was unforgivable. Did I hurt you badly?"

Maggie licked her dry lips and watched his sightless face, frozen with concern. She felt the air chilling her taut bareness where his warm, moist lips had left it vulnerable. "You didn't hurt me, Saxon," she confessed softly.

The hard lines of his face relaxed, and his hands swallowed her again, feeling her body tense and arch up to him as he explored it. "Still, I won't be that rough again," he promised. "Do you like the feel of my hands, Maggie?"

She fought for sanity, but he was creating unbelievable tension in her—new pleasures, exquisite pleasures. "Please," she breathed, reaching up to catch his head, to coax it down to her hungry body. "Like this. . . ."

"Yes, darling," he breathed, easing his mouth against her, "like this. . . ." He drew his forehead across her, his eyes, his cheeks, in a caress like nothing she'd ever imagined. For all her age she was remarkably innocent when it came to intimacy. Not because she was a prude, but simply because no man had ever stirred her blood the way Saxon was stirring it.

His lips touched her, adored her, in a silence that was intensified by the rustle of leaves in the breeze, the crispy sound of the leaves under her back as she writhed helplessly beneath his hands, his mouth.

He moved then, easing up to let her feel his full weight, from breast to thigh, and the unfamiliar differences between his male body and her own. She caught her breath at the sensation of oneness.

His mouth savored hers as his body moved sensuously over her own, faintly rocking, softly grinding, and she moaned helplessly.

"Nymph," he breathed into her mouth, his hands going under her slender hips to lift, gently, to press her to him. "Sweet little seductress, feel the effect you have on me."

"Saxon," she whispered achingly. "Oh, Saxon, what are you doing?"

"Don't be embarrassed," he whispered soothingly. "I know all too well how new this is for you. Just lie still, honey, and let me show you what to do. I'm going to be very, very slow, very tender. . . ." His hands moved and she bit off a tiny cry as she felt them easing the skirt up her smooth thighs.

"The road," she choked, feeling her crazy body yield to his, her legs cooperating with him, her hands clinging when they should be pushing, when his intention was too clear to mistake even for a novice.

He caught his own breath as he moved, creating a new, almost unbearable intimacy between them. Her body felt as if it were going to stiffen into oblivion, to die of the tension, arching endlessly upward, her fingers digging into his hips.

"Now," he breathed shakily, and his fingers found the buttons of his own shirt, opening it so that her breasts flattened under the warm, prickly weight of his hair-roughened chest. His body moved again, his hands touching her in unbearable ways. "Now, Maggie, help me. . . ."

It was the last straw. She gave in without reservation, loving him, wanting him, tears rolling down her cheeks at the painful hunger he was creating while she waited to give him everything, her body, her heart, her very soul. . . .

The sound of an approaching car barely penetrated her screaming mind, but Saxon heard it. Sensitive to the least interruption, despite his own staggering involvement, he lifted his head and froze. He was dragging at air, his body shuddering with mindless necessity, damp and faintly trembling, his heart shaking him.

"Oh, God, no," he ground out, and she watched his face contort as he dragged himself away from her to lie rigidly on his back. He looked like a man in unholy torment.

"Saxon, are you all right?" she asked quickly, dragging herself up hurriedly to rearrange her clothes, her eyes fearful as she stared at him and the car approached rapidly.

"What do you think?" he ground out.

His voice sounded ragged. She wondered at the wisdom of trying to fasten his shirt, but he was already doing it himself even as a carload of tourists came snaking past them on the highway. A woman in the passenger seat waved merrily, apparently oblivious to the blazing tension of the comfortable-looking people under the big maple tree.

"They're gone," she murmured unnecessarily.

He drew in one long final breath and sat up, his face dark and drawn. "Damn," he growled huskily. "Maggie, I almost took you, do you realize that? Right here, in plain view of the highway, and I was so far gone, I didn't even realize what I was trying to do!"

She studied his broad, hard face with faint awe. It was strangely satisfying to know she had that effect on him.

"You've been a long time without a woman, haven't you?" she asked haltingly.

His eyes began to glitter narrowly as he sat there, stiff and unyielding. "Is that what you think?" he asked sharply. "That I was so desperate, all I needed was a woman's body?"

"Wasn't it?" she asked, and held her breath for the answer.

The glitter got worse. "You really believe that I could use you like that, knowing you're a virgin?" He got to his feet. "Thanks for the character reading, Maggie. It's been fascinating. Let's go home."

"I wasn't trying to stop you," she reminded him quietly.

He laughed bitterly. "Of course not," he said with contempt. "Why should you? If I got you pregnant, I'd be wide open for a lawsuit. You'd be on easy street for life."

Her face went bone-white, but she didn't say a word. She started picking up the picnic things and loading them into the car, putting the trash in the trash cans. And she didn't say one word to him all the way back home.

When they got back, he was even worse, roaring around like a cyclone, growling about business, complaining about Maggie's lack of cooperation when she tried and failed to get a businessman he wanted to talk to on the phone for him. Finally she lost her temper and slammed out of his study, leaving him alone with his bad temper.

CHAPTER EIGHT

That evening she was careful to sit beside Lisa at the supper table and encouraged her to talk so that no one would notice her unusual quietness. At the head of the table Saxon looked no more disposed to conversation himself, brooding and darkly oblivious as he picked at his food.

Maggie escaped upstairs at the first possible minute, despite the fact that Saxon had gone straight to his study when the meal was finished. She couldn't face questions about the day she'd spent with her new boss without blushing, and that would have led to some interesting comments.

She sat in front of her mirror for a long time, brushing her hair with slow strokes while she relived every minute of his bruising, compelling ardor. It had been a long time since a man had tried to make love to her, and not once had she responded to another man the way she'd responded to Saxon. If the other car hadn't come barreling down the road, she'd have given in to him completely there under the trees, without even the thought of protest or modesty. She couldn't remember feeling such a blazing inferno of hunger. She still ached with it, burned with it. Just the memory of the afternoon made her body tingle with excitement. She'd loved the touch of his warm hard fingers on her skin, their expertise so evident that she bristled with envy for the women he'd learned it with. She closed her eyes and trembled with a silvery longing to be back in his arms again, to be cherished, to be . . . tutored. What would it be like to share his bed? she wondered hungrily, and her eyes flew open. She was going to have to get herself firmly in hand. An affair with Saxon Tremayne was a dead end, and she had the rest of her life to think about. Experiencing him as a lover would ruin her for any other man, and she didn't dare risk that. Life without him was going to be hard enough anyway, without that.

She thought ahead to the day she'd leave Jarrettsville, leave him, to go back to her job in Defiance. It was as bleak as winter to her mind. Just to sit and look at Saxon was pleasure enough for an entire day. To be touched by him was heaven itself.

She stood up, hating her weakness even as it washed her in yearning.

A sound caught her ears. She paused. It came again, louder, from the room next door that was occupied by Saxon. She hesitated for an instant before she went to it and stood listening.

It came again. A groan. A hard, rough groan, like that of a man in horrible pain, penetrated the thick wood.

She started to knock, then thought better of it. She opened the doorknob and pushed. It was unlocked.

She stepped into the brown-carpeted room, her eyes falling hungrily on Saxon's big body spread out on the thick quilted coverlet that was done in creams and browns to match the Mediterranean decor.

"Saxon?" she called softly.

He turned his head in the direction of her voice, and she could see harsh lines of pain carved into his pale face.

"Maggie?" he whispered huskily.

"Yes." She went to him, compassion softening her voice, and sat down gingerly on the bed beside him, feeling the warmth of his body radiating to her thigh. He was wearing trousers and his shirt, the jacket and tie thrown on a chair and his shoes sitting beside the bed.

His fingers felt across her thighs for her hand, in her lap, and he grasped it tightly. "Stay with me," he said in a taut tone. "I need you. God, I need you. . . ."

"I'll stay," she said soothingly. Her hand, unbidden, went to his broad forehead to brush back the disheveled silver-splintered darkness of his hair. His brow was hot to her cool fingers. "I'm right here; I won't go anywhere. What can I do to help? Is it a headache?"

"Damnable headache," he corrected, wincing. "Tablets—in the top drawer of the bedside table."

She let go of his hand and found the prescription bottle, reading the directions before she asked if he'd already taken any of them. When he shook his head, she toppled two of the white tablets into her palm and went to fetch a glass of water from the bathroom.

After he'd taken the tablets, he lay back heavily on the bed, his hair dark against the cream-colored pillowcase.

"It will take twenty minutes or so," she murmured. "I'm sorry; it must hurt abominably."

"What a tame word for it," he growled.

She smoothed his hair again, remembering his vicious words as they left the roadside park. Probably the headache had started then, and caused him to react to her the way he had. It was pain and frustration, not hatred, that had caused him to be so hostile. Now she understood, and the sting went away.

"I was damned cruel to you, wasn't I?" he asked curtly, as if he could hear the thoughts going through her mind.

"Yes, you were," she told him, not pulling her punches.

He managed a wan smile. "I wanted you," he said quietly. "The last thing in the world I expected was a carload of tourists to roar by."

She felt herself tingling at the thought of just when those tourists had interrupted them. "It was a pretty public place," she murmured.

"I didn't know where I was at the time, and don't pretend that you did either," he muttered. "You were just as involved as I was, and if they hadn't happened along, we'd have—"

"I'd have come to my senses," she replied curtly, trying to convince herself.

"Like hell you would've," he taunted.

She tried to smother a smile and lost. "Leave me a few illusions, will you?"

He laughed softly and sighed, pressing a hand against his forehead. "It was delicious, wasn't it?" he asked. "Just the two of us, no distractions, the wind blowing and the leaves rustling, and the taste of you in my mouth. . . ."

"If you're trying to embarrass me, forget it," she told him, fighting the urge to throw herself on him and kiss the breath out of him. "I'm twenty-six years old, and I don't think I can be shocked anymore."

"Do tell?" he murmured. "When I finally get you in my bed, we'll see about that. Or do you still have doubts that I'll manage that before you leave here?"

"I don't want to have an affair with you, Saxon," she said quietly. "That doesn't come under the terms of our agreement. I'm here to help you cope."

"And that's all?" He caught her fingers and raised them to his mouth, teasing their tips with his tongue, his lips, until she felt again the fiery longing to lie with him.

"How's your head?" she hedged, trying to ignore the sensations he was arousing.

"Getting better by the minute," he murmured. He pressed her palm against his mouth and traced its delicate lines with the tip of his tongue.

"You need rest. . . ."

"I need you," he breathed, tugging on her wrist. "Lie with me for a minute. Let me touch you the way I touched you this afternoon."

"We shouldn't. . . ." she protested.

"Maggie, we're both adults," he reminded her. "Grown-up people, not children playing with fire. We both know the risks, but I'm not going to take you like this. I'm far too tired to do you justice, and my head aches like hell. I just want to hold you against me. Is that so outrageous?"

"You make me sound like an adolescent prude,"

she grumbled. "And I'm not. I'm just cautious. I'm stupid about men and women in beds, hasn't that occurred to you? I don't even know how to protect myself, because I've never had to!"

"You don't have to now," he returned, glowering. "Not yet, at any rate. I won't seduce you tonight. Would you like that in writing and notarized?"

"I'd like to pour a bucket of hot oil over your head, that's what I'd like," she muttered venomously.

"It feels as if someone already has," he returned, and looked it.

She melted. It was diabolical of him to use his pain against her, but she couldn't refuse him.

"I can't believe this is good for you," she murmured as she eased down beside him on the bed.

He seemed to tense as he felt her body sliding alongside his, but after an instant, his arms slid around her and he moved, pillowing his heavy head against her warm breasts.

He sighed wearily. "Oh, God, that feels good," he whispered achingly.

Yes, it did, she thought, relaxing herself as the weight of his head made her feel the most exquisite pleasure. If it gave him peace, it was so little a sacrifice for her.

He relaxed there for a minute without moving, but almost inevitably, his lips began to inch forward, burning through her thin blouse as they found the slope of her breast.

"Saxon," she whispered.

He ignored the soft plea. "Don't talk," he murmured against her. His teeth nipped at her sensually through the layers of fabric that separated them. His

102

hands under her lifted, pressing her body hard against his mouth, and it became suddenly hungry, demanding.

She caught her breath. *Fool,* she taunted herself before she felt the first sensuous waves hit her. *Fool. You knew this would happen!*

He rolled over, taking her with him, so that she was lying on her back with his massive body above her while his mouth played relentlessly with her soft curves through the fabric.

"Help me undress you," he whispered against her throat. "I want to touch every inch of your skin with my lips."

"I want it too," she managed unsteadily. "But not like this—not now. Give me time, Saxon!"

"Why should I?"

Her eyes closed. "Because I've got to walk in with my eyes wide open," she said simply. "I've got to be willing to take the risks. I—I don't do things on the spur of the moment; I can't."

He laughed softly against her silken skin. "I told you not more than a minute ago that I wasn't going to seduce you. Didn't you hear me?"

"What would you call taking my clothes off?" she muttered.

"Exciting," he whispered wickedly. "Gloriously exciting. But I wasn't going to undress all of you, baby. Only the upper half—so that I can feel these," he whispered, brushing his lips maddeningly over her breasts, "deliciously bare."

She wanted that, too, with a surge of hunger that knocked her right off balance. Her body trembled

103

slightly, and he felt it, along with the almost imperceptible lifting of her body.

"We both want it," he breathed, halfway removing his weight so that his fingers could find the buttons.

"What are you doing to me, you sorcerer?" she accused with weak humor as she lay perfectly still and let him slowly, sensually, unfasten the buttons.

"Preparing you," he whispered just above her lips. "Getting you used to me, so that when the time finally comes for us, you won't be afraid to give yourself freely."

"Will the time . . . come for us?" she asked through taut lips as she felt his expert fingers toying with the front clasp that held the lacy wisp of her bra together.

"Inevitably," he replied in a slow, tender tone. "It's been building since the day we met. You haven't missed me any less than I've missed you."

Her eyes went liquid. "Have you . . . missed me?" she asked.

"More than I can tell you," he replied. He unfastened the clip and slowly eased the fabric away, so that she was bare from the waist up, so that the faint chill of the room washed over her, emphasizing her lack of clothing. "But not," he breathed, his fingers poised over her, "more than I can show you. God, Maggie, I wish I could see you," he ground out.

"There's very little to see," she whispered lightly, aching for his touch on her body in a warm, sweet yielding.

His fingers lowered, and she trembled as they made contact with the taut peak, very tenderly tracing it, and the softness surrounding it, while his face seemed to harden and go rigid.

"You want this very much, don't you?" he asked, confident of her response because of the things the reactions of her traitorous body were telling him.

"Can't you feel that?" she asked on a gasp.

"I can feel it," he agreed tautly. "But I want to hear it. I'm not used to making love blind, Maggie. This is the first time I've touched a woman since it happened."

"Is it very different from being in a dark room?" she asked unsteadily.

He bent over her, and his mouth smiled against her lips. "Maggie," he breathed as he took her mouth, "I've never made love in the dark."

Before that soft taunt could register, he was kissing her, and touching her, and her body was lifting in unholy torment to beg for the slow, lazy fingers that were introducing it to such exquisite pleasure.

She wondered how a human body could survive this kind of torture—aching with hunger, burning with a fever that no amount of ice could soothe, wanting. Wanting!

"Don't cry," he whispered, holding her still against him, his hands at her back, soothing, his mouth gently touching all over her face as he brought her down from the wildness of the plateau they'd reached together.

She couldn't seem to stop trembling, and pressed closer, drawing his strength into her. "Saxon," she moaned.

"It's all right, honey," he whispered softly. "Calm down now. It's all right."

Her arms clung around his neck. "Is it always like this?" she asked with a ghost of a laugh. "Do people go crazy like this, until they're on fire and burning up?"

His fingers smoothed back her wild hair. "It usually takes a lot more than what we did to cause that kind of reaction, Maggie," he said at her ear. His lips brushed the lobe. "I barely touched you," he breathed.

"I know." She laughed nervously.

His arms contracted, swallowing her closely. "God, you're sweet," he ground out, rocking her roughly. "Sweet, like honey, to taste, to kiss. You make me want to curl up with the pleasure."

She sighed into his thick hair. "There couldn't have been much of that, for you," she murmured. "I don't even know how to touch you."

His breath seemed to catch. "It boggles the mind," he murmured.

She nuzzled her face against his. "How's your headache?"

"What headache?" he chuckled.

She smiled, closing her eyes. They seemed to fit together beautifully, despite the disparity in their sizes, as if she had been created for him.

"Sleep with me," he whispered, tightening his arms. "Go and put on your gown and sleep with me, all night."

She wanted to. Her body screamed for it. But her practical mind reared its ugly head.

"No," she said gently.

"Why?"

She smiled wistfully. "Because we wouldn't sleep."

He chuckled at her ear. "Probably not. But, honey, it's going to happen. The only question is when, not if."

She knew that too. If she stayed here, it was inevitable. And how could she possibly leave him? It had been agony the last time; she'd never have the strength until he actually sent her away. And no matter what his motives were, it wouldn't make any difference. She was too hungry for him to care—that was the really frightening thought.

"Then not tonight," she whispered.

"All right," he agreed after a minute, and his arms tightened for an instant before he let her go. "Not tonight."

She sat up, putting herself back together. "Can I get you anything else before I turn in?"

He shook his head. "I'll be all right now. I want you to drive me down to Bilings Sportswear in the morning," he said suddenly, his face faintly brooding. "I've got to clear up that mess before I do one other thing."

It was good to see him involving himself in business again, she thought, and felt a stirring of pride at having been partially responsible.

"All right," she said. "What time would you like to leave?"

"Nine o'clock," he said. "I'll see you downstairs at seven." He grinned. "I'll touch you downstairs at seven," he amended.

"Why, you lecherous thing," she gasped.

He cocked an eyebrow. "You let me touch you up here. What's different about downstairs?"

"I'm going to bed before you compromise my principles," she informed him, rising.

"That might be wise. Maggie!" he called as she opened the connecting door.

"Yes?" she turned expectantly.

He started to say something and apparently thought better of it, because his face closed up. "Nothing. Good night, honey, sleep well. And thanks for the . . . sympathy."

"Not at all," she grinned. "Thanks for the . . . instruction."

"As the saying goes," he murmured, "you ain't seen nothin' yet."

"That's what scares me," she murmured, and with a soft good night, quickly closed the door.

He was cheerful and pleasant at breakfast for a change, looking rested and sexy and altogether too attractive in a brown pin-striped vested suit that gave him a tigerish appearance. Probably that was deliberate, too, she thought, but wondered absently how he'd picked out the color when he was blind.

"It's simple," he returned when she asked him, "I had Mother buy some of those plastic puzzles for infants. I put a different shape on each color. Square is gray." He chuckled. "Triangle is brown, circle is blue, and so forth."

"You," she said, "are a genius."

His white teeth flashed for an instant. "I try, baby, I try. What are you wearing?"

"A gray skirt, a white blouse, and a navy-blue blazer with black accessories," she replied.

"What does the blouse look like?" he asked with a raised eyebrow. "Is it low-cut?"

"I'll have you know, I'm dressed very conservatively," she returned. "The blouse has a modest V neck slashed to the waist, and the skirt has a slit all the way up to my thigh."

He chuckled delightedly. "Try again."

"Well, actually the blouse has a jabot collar, and the skirt only has a kick pleat in back," she told him. "But my wrists are shamelessly exposed," she added in a whisper.

"Brazen hussy," he accused.

"Only in bed with sexy men," she retorted.

"Only then if they teach you what to do," he accused.

"Well, I'm learning," she said defensively.

"Whew!" he said wickedly. "Are you ever!"

She grinned and picked up her fork. The ham and eggs looked delicious.

Bilings Sportswear was located on the outskirts of Spartanburg, a nice medium-sized company with over two hundred employees. It was strictly a manufacturing company, not a vertical-mill operation like the Tremayne Corporation. But it boasted a level of quality that any corporation would be proud to claim.

Its neat cutting room featured a conveyor belt to carry the huge bales of cloth to the stockroom, and long tables where spreaders and cutters worked to produce the pattern cloth pieces that were assembled on the shirt and pants lines by hardworking seam-stresses. Everywhere there was the sound of sewing machines, a loud hum that drowned conversation. Conveyor belts were installed in both divisions, running between the sewing machine operators to carry piece goods in baskets as they passed through each operation in their assembly into clothes.

The office was a bright cheerful place with smiling women who did payroll and reception work and nattily dressed executives in suits who worked at administrative tasks and public relations.

Maggie was fascinated with the plant. Textiles had been one of her interests long before Saxon Tremayne stormed into her life, and the process of clothes-making had never bored her.

She clung to Saxon's big warm hand as the plant vice-president Gordy Kemp escorted them through the operation. He was a tall man, very slender, with small green eyes and a thin smile that was all too ready.

Maggie couldn't help remembering what she'd heard about the man in Saxon's office.

"I'd like to have all the workers assembled in the shirt line now," Saxon said curtly when the tour was finished and they were standing at the swinging doors that separated the plant from the offices.

"Now?" Kemp burst out.

"Right now," was the cold reply.

Kempt shrugged, looked vaguely uneasy, and went into the office to have the announcement made over the plant's intercom.

Saxon's fingers tightened on Maggie's. "Stay right beside me," he said in her ear.

"What are you going to do?"

"Wait and see." His dark eyes gleamed with challenge and something else.

The sewing machines gradually came to a halt and the employees slowly grouped into a semicircle facing the doors where Saxon, Maggie, and the young Kemp were standing.

Kemp looked more nervous than ever. "They're all here, Mr. Tremayne," he told the older man.

Saxon nodded. "Good morning," he began, addressing the workers, raising his deep voice so that it carried with a faint echo through the cavernous plant. "For the benefit of those who don't know me—and very likely that means most of you—I'm Saxon Tremayne. My corporation is in the process of absorbing Bilings Sportswear, as you've no doubt heard by now."

There was a low murmur among the employees that sounded faintly antagonistic.

"I understand," Saxon continued calmly, "that some of you are under the misconception that my immediate priority is the dismissal of the older employees here on some kind of trumped-up excuse."

That almost brought the house down. Kemp tugged at his necktie. "Mr. Tremayne . . ." he began in a strangled whisper.

Saxon raised a curt hand, stopping him. "I also understand," he added, "that this misconception has been promoted by certain management personnel within this organization."

Kemp stiffened, and Maggie glanced away before he noticed her interest.

"I want you all to know that we have no intention

whatsoever of trying to cheat our older employees out of their well-deserved retirement benefits," Saxon said firmly, lifting his face as if he were staring straight at the onlookers. "Indeed, you may expect an immediate raise in salaries, increased insurance benefits, and paid holidays. All of which I was amazed to learn that you *weren't* already getting. How does that sound?"

There was a loud roar, a lot of laughter, and some whistles. Saxon grinned. "I thought you might like that. And you senior employees will be interested to learn that we also plan to increase your retirement benefits.

"Here's what's going to happen within the next two weeks. Our administrative people have been working with Bilings's executives to formulate some new company policies. One of them is going to include monthly listening sessions—bull sessions, if you prefer. Two days a month you'll have the opportunity to sit down and talk with a designated executive if you have any complaints or suggestions for improvements. We're also installing a suggestions box, so that you can gripe and suggest improvements between listening sessions. Any improvements we implement because of an employee's suggestion will result in a nice bonus for the employee who suggested it.

"We're also going to update the operation here—add some new equipment and replace some of the older machinery."

There was a hush in the big room, and Kemp looked as if he were searching out a hole to jump into.

"Any complaints so far?" Saxon asked dryly.

"No!" several employees chorused, followed by another roar of laughter.

Saxon grinned. "That's just the beginning. I'll have more to say on the subject of changes later, and notices will be posted on the bulletin boards. When we get some of these improvements going, we'll have another plant-wide meeting and review what's been accomplished. Meanwhile if any of you has any reservations about the takeover, I want to know it. And from now on," he added darkly, "if you hear any rumors, bring them straight to me. I'll get to the bottom of it, and the perpetrator is going to find himself in a hell of a fix.

"One more thing," he added. "I'm not offering you any handouts. These added benefits aren't a bribe to keep you sweet. They're an advance against your continued attention to detail and your pride in production of a superior line of clothing. I understand that the quality-control people here are bored to death because they can hardly find enough seconds, thirds, and wash garments to keep them working. That says a hell of a lot for you people, and I appreciate it. That's why you're getting raises. And if you keep putting out that kind of work, the raises will keep coming. If I make money, you make money, and later on we'll even discuss some stock-sharing programs. Now let's all get back to work."

With a rumble of happy, startled conversation the employees began to disperse, while Maggie watched with a faint smile and shook her head in bewilderment.

"Kemp?" Saxon asked curtly.

The young executive cleared his throat uncomfortably. "Yes, Mr. Tremayne?"

"Come into the office with me. You and I have a little business to discuss."

Saxon allowed Maggie to help him into the office and seat himself behind the big desk. "Okay, honey," he told her, "go read a magazine or something. I'll only be a few minutes."

"Okay," she grinned.

It was several minutes before the door to the office opened, and Kemp came out, his face pale. Maggie put down the magazine she'd been reading and went inside to help Saxon find his way back out.

"Now take me down to the cutting room," he told Maggie. He looked big and confident and faintly triumphant, and not the least embarrassed about letting her guide him around. It was such a change from their first encounter since his blindness that she smiled.

"What did you do to him?" she asked as they walked down the long, wide aisle past the smiling women on the assembly line. "He rushed straight out the front door."

"I put him in charge of the order department," he told her, "and sent him off to lunch. The cutting-room foreman has been here for twenty years, and he's been consistently passed over for promotion because of a disagreement he had with management over salaries. Apparently he's the only department head on the place who wasn't afraid to complain about the low pay."

"Going to pat him on the back?" she teased.

"I'm going to give him Kemp's job," he said, smiling. "I need a man I can trust running things here, and he's the shop foreman's friend as well. Always remember, honey, if you delegate, be damned sure of your choices. A bad manager can cost you an arm, figuratively speaking."

"Is there a union here?" she asked. "You mentioned a shop foreman, but—"

"There's a union forming," he replied. "The employees got desperate enough to vote it in, and even though I'm in management, after reviewing the operation here, I can't honestly say I blame them."

"Will Mr. Kemp stay on, do you think?"

"I don't know. He's been here for six years, Maggie, I couldn't just boot him out the door without giving him a chance. He's young yet, and making mistakes, but he's got the opportunity to learn if he takes it." He frowned. "Are we anywhere near the cutting room?"

"Just about. I've got homing pigeon instincts," she added with a grin, squeezing the big hand she was holding as they turned the corner into the cutting room. "Trust me."

"I'm beginning to see one of the benefits of this damned shrapnel," he said with a faint smile. "I get to hold hands with you all the time."

"You could do that if you weren't blind," she said.

"Could I really?" His voice was quiet and deep. "Or would you pack up and run if I regained my sight? You're a lot less nervous of me now than you were when I could see, Maggie."

She moved closer to his side, feeling a surge of warmth that made her want to throw her arms around him and hold tight. "When you had your sight," she reminded him, "you could have had any woman you wanted."

He drew in a sharp breath. "My God, you don't think I'd want you if I could see? And you say *I'm* blind!"

She looked up, wanting to pursue that, when a big, husky man with red hair came walking toward them from the office nearby.

"Morning," he said pleasantly, going to pass them.

"Good morning," Saxon replied. "Can you tell me where to find Red Halley?"

The other man, every bit Saxon's size, grinned. "You just did."

Saxon stretched out his hand toward the man's voice. "I'm Saxon Tremayne."

"Glad to meet you," Red said with a firm handshake. "That was a nice speech you made."

"It wasn't just a speech," Saxon said quietly. "I meant every word. How would you feel about ramrodding this operation for me?"

Red looked as if he'd tried to swallow a watermelon. "Me?"

"Mr. Kemp has just accepted the position of head order clerk. I'm offering you his old job."

"Why?" Red burst out.

"Because you're a fighter," he replied. "I admire courage, Mr. Halley. I like executives who don't dive under their desks when I start raising hell about production. I don't think you will."

"But I never finished technical school," came the protest. "I lack three quarters—"

"There's an excellent technical school less than ten miles away," Saxon said, unabashed. "I'll foot the bill while you complete your training at night school."

Red sighed. "I'll have to accept now, won't I?" he asked with a sheepish grin.

"Don't bother to thank me," Saxon interrupted when the other man started to do just that. "You'll earn every penny you get."

"When do I start?"

"How soon can you get to the office?" Saxon asked. "Hand over your job to the man you feel is best qualified to replace you. Now I've got to get going. I've a pretty full schedule. Good luck."

Red shook hands with him again and went off looking thunderstruck.

"Shall we go, Maggie?" Saxon asked after a minute.

She caught his hand and led him off toward the rear exit of the building. "I just stand in awe of you, Mr. Corporation Executive," she told him. "Talk about grit."

"You're not exactly lacking in that department yourself, wildcat." He chuckled. "Shall I wave goodbye to the girls as I go out the door?"

"It wouldn't be good business," she assured him. "They're already drooling over you, you gorgeous hunk. If you give them any encouragement, you'll be mobbed on the way out."

He cocked an eyebrow. "Oh? Are they pretty?"

"Every last blessed one of them," she grumbled, and meant it—even the plumper employees had attractive, smiling faces.

"Hmmm." He laughed delightedly and put his

arm around her, drawing her close. "Jealous, honey?"

"Murderously," she agreed, going along with him.

"I wish that was the truth," he said quietly, and his arm contracted. "But I suppose I expect too much. Take me home, Maggie," he added before she could ask him what he meant.

"Have you ever considered writing a book on textile management?" she asked on the way home.

"A book? I've done articles," he admitted. "But not a book."

"It might be an interesting project," she suggested. "The market isn't flooded with them, and you've been in the business for quite some time."

He leaned his dark head back against the seat with a frown. He felt in his pocket for a cigarette and lighted it. "My God, you're full of surprises," he murmured. "I seem to have come back to life since you got here."

"I'll agree with that," she said. "But all you needed was a prod. You aren't the type of man to sit down and go to seed."

"Are you so sure of that?" he asked. "If you'll remember, I've done very little for the past few months."

She stopped at a traffic light on the outskirts of Jarrettsville. "Perhaps it was all that concerned kindness that clogged you up," she teased. "You just needed a nurse who'd hit you over the head with a brick twice a day."

He laughed. "What a way to treat a poor blind man!"

"You? Poor? Blind?" she exclaimed.

"A man at least, surely," he murmured.

She grinned, watching the light go green. "I've never had any doubts on that score."

"Especially at certain times?" he murmured.

She was glad he couldn't see the color in her cheeks. "You ought to be ashamed of yourself," she commented. "Trying to seduce innocent women in public places."

"As I recall, I almost made it too."

"I can't deny that," she admitted quietly. "I was more than willing. And I hope you aren't going to take advantage of that," she added. "I can't help the way I respond to you. I'm too new at it to be very good at restraint. Especially when you're offering me a kind of pleasure I've never experienced."

His hand felt across the seat to catch hers and clasp it warmly. "That's one thing I've always liked about you," he said gently. "Your total lack of guile. You never lie to me, even when it embarrasses you to tell the truth."

"Wouldn't you know the difference?" she asked warmly.

"I think I would," he murmured. He sighed and squeezed her hand. "All right, I'll do my best not to back you into any corners. But I want you desperately. Surely you know that?"

"Yes," she said. "I know."

"Men are notoriously shrewd when their emotions take over. I wouldn't consciously make you give in—but I can't promise that I won't ever lose my head. You've already had blatant proof that I'm not always in perfect control of myself."

119

"Do you really want . . . just me, and not just a woman?" she asked, needing reassurance.

"You asked me that once before, and I blew up," he recalled. "No, Maggie, I don't just want a warm body. And even if I did, I've too much respect for you to use you that way. Satisfied?"

"I reckon," she drawled. Her eyes slid sideways to study his face. If his life was changing, so was hers. She felt a part of him, a very necessary part. He wasn't the kind of man who'd ever need another human being when he was all in one piece. He was self-sufficient and stubbornly independent. But now, without his sight, he was necessarily dependent on Maggie, and she loved being necessary to him—even in a small way.

"How are you at taking dictation?" he asked suddenly.

"Oh, I think I can keep up with you," she assured him, "if you still dictate the way you used to."

"Are you willing to stay with me until I finish the book?" he persisted. "I'd hate to have to break in a new typist after the first chapter or two; it wouldn't be good for the continuity."

She thought about that. Her newspaper job was important to her—it had been the most important thing in her life. But now there was Saxon. And if it came down to a choice, there really wasn't one. She'd call her boss and explain and hope he'd hold her job. If he couldn't, well, there was always nearby Ashton. She could find another job doing something. . . .

"I'll stay with you," she said quietly.

He lifted his cigarette to his lips and looked darkly

120

relieved. "We'll start today then. It'll give me something to do."

That had been her plan at the outset, but she wasn't going to admit it to him. It was enough that he'd snapped up the bait, Maggie thought.

They spent the afternoon in his study while he got his thoughts together and outlined the basic proposal for her. They decided between them what information would be needed besides his own expertise, and she took dictation for letters to be sent out to acquire the additional information.

Lisa waylaid her on the way upstairs as they went to clean up before supper.

"How's it going?" she asked Maggie. "I haven't heard him yell all afternoon."

"He hasn't," Maggie said, and grinned. "Oh, Lisa, if you'd seen him this morning at the plant! He was just fabulous. Took over the place, charmed the employees, displaced a scheming executive—he was wonderful!"

"He seems a lot different these days," her sister replied softly. "Of course, you've got a long way to go."

"Don't remind me!" Maggie laughed. "But I've made a start. At least now he's got something to do besides brood."

"That's a fact. By the way," Lisa added, stopping at the door to Maggie's room, "did you know that Sandra's invited guests for supper?"

Maggie's eyebrows lifted. "Who?"

Lisa sighed. "The girl next door and her brother, I'm afraid," she said gently, watching Maggie's face fall. "She's not very happy about it either; they stopped by and practically invited themselves. There was nothing she could do—graciously—except agree to it." Lisa's eyes clouded with anger. "The girl's name is Marlene Aikens, and her brother is Bret. He's okay, but she's a fourteen-karat pain in the neck."

"Does Saxon know?" Maggie asked.

"I doubt it. Sandra said Marlene chased him relentlessly until he all but threw her out the front door. But she's getting brave again. Figured that absence would make the heart grow fonder." Lisa grinned. "Sandra doesn't think so though."

Maggie only nodded. But she had a strangely disquieting feeling about the dinner party—as if it might develop into something that would drastically affect her happiness.

CHAPTER NINE

It was just as well that Saxon couldn't see, Maggie thought miserably, sitting across from Marlene Aikens at the long elegant table. She'd only have felt more dowdy than she looked, compared to the elegant blonde's simple and wildly expensive black sheath dress. Maggie's plum-colored pantsuit was like something off the rack by comparison, and the older woman's sophisticated smile let her know it.

But Bret Aikens was a pleasant man, just Maggie's age, with dark hair and eyes and an easygoing personality—nothing like that of his rather flamboyant sister. Maggie found herself seated next to him at the table, and they had an immediate rapport.

"I hear you've become Saxon's eyes," he murmured over the salad.

She smiled. "In a matter of speaking," she confided. "And not totally. There are times and places when he has to make a guess. . . ."

He grinned. "Say no more. You're from Georgia?"

"Sure am," she said pleasantly. "But I enjoy your state. It's beautiful country up here."

"We think so," he nodded. "Of course, the low country is the most densely populated, and with

Charleston and Myrtle Beach and Hilton Head and those resort places, it tends to draw more attention. But our chamber of commerce is trying to devote more time to promote the upcountry now."

"The history is what fascinates me," Maggie said, sipping her coffee. "I was never all that interested in the Revolutionary War, but since I've been here, I'm getting curious."

"You'll find that more Revolutionary War battles and skirmishes were fought in South Carolina than in any other state," he told her. "Around a hundred and thirty-seven of them, if memory serves."

"So many?" she exclaimed.

"You bet. And did you know that General Frances Marion—the so-called Swamp Fox—was from South Carolina?"

She laughed. "How could I forget? He's my father's hero. My father," she added, "is a history professor at our local college. Which helps to explain my interest in the subject. It was self-defense!"

He smiled across the table at her, and there was pure male interest in his eyes. "What a dull subject for such a pretty girl," he murmured.

She pursed her lips. "What a silver tongue you have, sir. Do you polish it daily?"

He tossed her a roguish wink. "Twice every day," he agreed.

Down the table Saxon was being treated to a breathy recital of Marlene's "utterly boring" week. He didn't seem to mind though. His broad face was smiling as he listened.

"The worst part of it all has been missing you, darling." She was sighing, putting a well-manicured hand on his broad one where it was resting on the table. "Why wouldn't you let me visit you?"

"I've been busy," Saxon replied. "And now that Maggie's here to help me get around, I'm going to be even busier. We're working on a very interesting project together."

"Oh?" Marlene asked with a venomous look in Maggie's direction. "What, darling?"

"That," Saxon murmured dryly, "would be telling. Wouldn't it, Maggie?"

"Yes, it would," she said, nodding, and gave Marlene a fearless grin.

"Well, how mysterious." Marlene laughed coldly. "But could I borrow you tomorrow, Saxon, for an hour or so? I've been so lonely. . . ."

"Sorry, Marlene," he replied without hesitation. "I told you, I'm going to be on a tight schedule for a while."

"Business, always business." The blonde pouted. "You never let yourself have any fun."

"Don't I?" Saxon murmured with a tiny smile, and Maggie fought to keep from blushing.

The conversation drifted inevitably to the coming holiday season, and Sandra elaborated on her plans for Lisa and Randy's Christmas wedding.

"If you have time later this week," Bret murmured to Maggie, "I'd love to drive you over to Spartanburg and show you the Price House and the Walnut Grove Plantation. They both date back to the eighteenth century. In fact, the Walnut Grove Manor House dates back to seventeen sixty-five and was the home of a female scout for the Revolutionary War generals at the Battle of Cowpens. Come to think of

125

it," he added with a beaming smile, "we could drive over to the Cowpens National Battlefield while we're at it and see where the Patriots gave the Redcoats their worst defeat. . . ."

"I'd love to," she said, interrupting him. "What day?"

"Friday? About eight thirty, and we'll make an early start?"

She nodded. "That will be fine. And—uh—don't mention it to Saxon just yet, will you? I'd rather tell him myself."

He studied her and glanced down the table to the big dark man. "He won't like it," he sighed.

"I know," she murmured with a mischievous smile.

"He doesn't even make you nervous, does he? He frightens most people."

"The bigger they are, et cetera," she assured him.

"If you say so," he said grinning. "But just in case, we might see if we could get one of those old cannons in my trunk. . . . say, did you know that the old Confederates used walnut hulls to dye their uniforms gray? They took the—"

"—those black walnuts in the big yucky hulls that dye your shoes black when you walk over them?" she interrupted.

"The very same," he agreed, and proceeded to tell her how the dyeing process was accomplished.

She listened with obvious interest. He was so different from his snobby sister. She liked him. And she had a feeling that she was going to need that day away from the house. It looked as if Saxon were planning to put a lot of work into the book. That

126

would mean a lot of work for her, she thought—not that she minded. It was just that she dreaded the enforced proximity with him. She was uncertain of her powers of resistance if he began to put on pressure. She didn't think she could survive an affair with him. Bret, on the other hand, was a nice safe man with no evil intentions who could be her shield against Saxon's ardor. At least she hoped he could. And she had a feeling that she was going to need one.

The next two days went by smoothly and with surprising speed. Saxon dictated, Maggie wrote and typed, and work on the manuscript progressed nicely.

On the third day they worked right through supper, eating on trays in his study, where they locked themselves so that they wouldn't be interrupted by the rest of the family.

"Getting tired?" he asked after they'd finished eating and Maggie had taken ten more pages of dictation.

She stretched lazily. "Not terribly. Are you?"

He leaned back in the swivel chair behind his desk, his powerful chest muscles emphasized by the long-sleeved beige silk shirt he was wearing as he lifted his arms. "I very rarely feel the need for rest this early," he confessed. "I enjoy working. I like what I do."

"And that's probably why you've made such a success of it," she remarked. Her eyes studied his hard, deeply lined face. "Saxon, haven't you ever wanted a family of your own?" she asked suddenly.

He laughed shortly. "What brought that on?"

"I don't know," she admitted. "It's something I've wondered about, that's all."

His eyes darkened as his head turned toward the sound of her voice. "I could ask you the same question."

She smiled wistfully. "Yes, I'd like a home and children of my own. It just never happened for me. I'd have to love a man very much to consider living the rest of my life with him."

"And you've never loved anyone like that?" he probed.

She shrugged "I've thought I was in love once or twice," she said softly, not adding that one of those times was with him, and that she still felt that way.

He sat very still, his whole posture attentive. "And?"

"It didn't work out" was all she'd admit to. "And you?"

He leaned back in his chair. "I found the woman I wanted," he said harshly. "I just couldn't keep her."

She was suddenly and violently jealous of the faceless woman, but she schooled her voice not to show it. Her hands clasped each other tightly in her lap.

"Did it . . . have something to do with your blindness?" she asked quietly.

"Everything," he growled.

And for that, he blamed her. He didn't have to say it; it was in the hard lines of his face, in his sharp half-angry tone. And what could she do? Nothing would restore his sight, according to what he'd told her.

"Have you thought about going back to see your doctor?" she asked after a minute.

"What for?" he asked wearily. "The problem is a piece of shrapnel, Maggie. Unless it miraculously shifts from its present position, there's nothing to be done; they've already told me that." He got up from the chair and felt his way around the edge of the desk and to the sofa where Maggie was sitting rigidly on the edge of her seat.

"Where are you?" he asked, reaching out a big hand slowly.

She caught his fingers and curled hers around them. "I'm right here," she said, and her eyes adored him.

His own fingers moved, wrapping themselves warmly around hers, and he smiled. "How long has it been since I've kissed you?"

"Oh, a lifetime or so," she returned lightly. But her heart was racing, her breath was catching, and her eyes were on his broad mouth with an aching hunger.

"Too much work and too little play isn't good for either one of us, you know," he said softly.

"So they say," she replied in a breathless tone.

His fingers tightened. He leaned back against the sofa. His free hand flicked open the buttons of his shirt lazily, and a slow, sensual smile touched his mouth.

"Suppose you come here," he murmured deeply, "and I'll give you a refresher course in basic lust?"

She laughed helplessly. "Why, you lecherous old tycoon, you!"

He sobered, his eyes narrowing. "Maggie, do I

really seem old to you?" he asked suddenly, and as if it mattered.

Her heart ached for him. She felt a tinge of regret for the thoughtless teasing. "No," she said softly, easing down into his warm, hard arms to pillow her cheek against his hair-roughened chest. "No, you don't seem old to me at all. Just mature and sensuous, and quite deliciously masculine."

He caught his breath. His hand pressed her cheek against the warm muscles, moving it slowly, rhythmically against him. His breathing quickened at the feel of her skin; his heart thundered at her ear. "Sensuous?" he murmured huskily.

"Very," she admitted, and felt her own breath becoming ragged. She liked the feel of the curling hair, faintly abrasive at her eyes, against her nose, against the corner of her mouth. Her lips parted and she moved, turning them against his chest, enjoying the tangy scent of soap and cologne and pure man in her nostrils as she breathed him. His hands caught in her hair, tangling in it as if he enjoyed its silky texture, and he brought her lips against him in a slow circular pattern.

She let him guide her mouth, tasting him as she felt the hard edge of his belt against her cheek, her hands enjoying the rough warmth of his chest in a silence that burned with sweet sensation.

Her fingers tangled in the wiry hair over the warm muscles, testing its strength as she drew back to look at him.

His hand touched her face, long fingers tracing her eyes, her eyebrows, her nose and cheeks and chin and the soft line of her mouth.

130

"I wish I could see you," he murmured softly, his voice deep and quiet in the stillness of the room. "You're very quiet when I hold you—your voice gives away nothing until I arouse you completely."

She buried her face in his warm throat, touched by the words, by the softness of his voice. "Can't you tell that you please me?" she whispered.

"I don't want to know what you're feeling," he murmured. "Your body tells me that. I want to know what you're thinking."

"Why?"

His fingers moved down to her neck, catching in the softness of her hair to ease her head back on his chest, arching her throat.

"Your heart's going faster by the second," he remarked quietly. His fingers slipped down to the soft, firm roundness of her breast and cupped it as if she were already his possession.

"So is yours," she whispered back shakily.

He bent, his mouth brushing hers gently. "Lie with me," he whispered, easing her down with him on the sofa. "Let's make love to each other and forget the world and the darkness. Let's forget everything . . . except this. . . ."

His mouth took hers, warm and hard and frankly hungry, his arms bending her into the hard contours of his body while the kiss went on and on.

Vaguely she felt his hands under the soft T-shirt she was wearing, lifting it, finding the small clasp that held her bra together and unfastening it with slow deft hands.

"Saxon . . ." she protested weakly.

"Let me," he whispered, finding her with his hands. "You know you want to."

Of course, she did; that was the whole trouble, Maggie thought. Denying herself the magic of his touch on her bare skin was as impossible as denying she loved him.

His mouth brushed lazily, teasingly, across hers. "Take it off," he murmured.

"The family—"

"The door's locked, remember?" he whispered, half amused. "And I can't see you. . . ."

What good did protesting matter anyway? she wondered dimly as his hands went to work, easing the top and the bra from her before he laid her gently back down on the soft cushions.

He started to move down, but she pushed gently at his own shirt with hands that should have been protesting, not helping him.

"Do you want it off?" he asked tautly, his usual control oddly faltering

"Please," she whispered.

He stripped off the shirt and tossed it onto the carpet, and she caught her breath at the size of his chest and shoulders, the huge muscular arms and the arrowing of dark hair that ran down surely past his belted waist.

"Do you like what you see?" he asked under his breath as he eased down so that she could feel only the warmth of his torso but not its touch.

"Oh, yes," she whispered, and her eyes worshipped him. "Yes, I like it very much."

"I wish I could look at you," he breathed gruffly, easing slowly, slowly down so that she felt him first as a whisper then, with tormenting pleasure, felt the abrasive masculinity that teased and stirred her body until it told him blatantly how much it wanted his.

His mouth was tender on her face while his fingers, softly touching and exploring textures, sought and found the proof of her arousal.

"Do I feel as good to you as you feel to me?" he asked in a curt undertone.

"Yes," she breathed into his mouth.

His hands moved down to her narrow hips, bringing them sensuously against his, grinding them against him slowly. She moaned softly, and he caught the tiny sound under his mouth, smothering it. His tongue teased her lips and darted into her mouth; she felt her body go rigid with desire and wondered how it could bear the tension of wanting and not having.

He whispered barely intelligible words into her ears, endearments mingled with remarks that made her skin burn and her body tingle.

"Am I shocking you?" he laughed breathlessly as his body moved completely over hers, letting her feel the powerful contours crushing her down into the soft cushions.

"Yes, you beast, you are," she gasped, trying without success to catch her breath as his hips moved against hers with shattering intimacy.

"Don't just lie under me," he ground out. "Help me."

Her nails dug into his powerful arms. "Saxon, don't," she pleaded shakily as the unfamiliar intimacy made her tremble. "Please, don't."

"I want you," he replied tautly. "And what's

more, you want me. Do you think I can't feel it, taste it?"

"Not . . . like this," she pleaded, knowing that if she didn't reach him soon, she never would. "Please!"

His breath was coming heavily and hard. He hesitated, his sightless eyes looking down as if trying to see her. "Is it the setting that bothers you?" he growled. "We could go up to my bedroom, or yours."

"You know why," she whispered.

His jaw tautened. "I know you're a virgin, if that's what you mean. I won't hurt you, Maggie."

"You only want me because you're blind," she shot at him, desperate for ammunition, and hated the words when she felt him stiffen. "That's all it is, Saxon. You want me because I'm a woman and I'm handy!"

His face darkened angrily. He pushed himself away from her and sat up, so sensuously attractive that it was all she could do not to throw herself on him. But she gritted her teeth and put her bra and blouse back on, avoiding looking at him.

"Hand me my shirt," he said curtly, as if he hated having to ask her even for that.

She put it into his outstretched hand and turned away when he pulled it back on.

She heard the click of his lighter as he lighted a cigarette and smelled the acrid smoke a minute later.

"You wanted me enough that night in my room," he said with biting sarcasm. "What happened, Maggie? Did you suddenly get turned off by my loss of sight, or did your dinner partner have something to do with it?"

"Dinner partner?" she murmured, remembering Bret and the invitation she was going to have to own up to.

"Bret Aikens," he reminded her.

"He's very nice," she said noncommittally.

"Mother said you and Bret had a lot of common interests," he said shortly.

She sighed. "Well, we both like history," she admitted. "In fact, he's taking me to Spartanburg tomorrow to see some special points of interest there," she added defiantly.

His face went livid. She could see miniature explosions in his eyes. "Like hell he is," he said. "You've got work to do!"

"Not tomorrow I haven't," she told him. "I'm going."

"Not while you're working for me!"

She threw back her hair and started toward the door. "I'm either going to Spartanburg tomorrow or I'm going home to Georgia tomorrow," she shot back at him from the safety of the doorway. "And there isn't one thing you can do to stop me!"

She went out, slamming the door noisily behind her.

Saxon wasn't up when Bret came to pick her up promptly at eight thirty the next morning, and Maggie breathed a sigh of relief. She'd really been prepared to pack her bag and go home if she'd had trouble about the trip, but she was secretly glad that she didn't have to carry out the threat. Leaving

Saxon now was going to be worse than having a tooth pulled without anesthetic, and no doubt it would hurt for a long time.

But she schooled herself to forget the future and concentrate on one day at a time. Bret was good company, keeping up a pleasant, undemanding conversation as they headed down to catch one interstate going east and another going south.

"We'll bypass Spartanburg on the way down to Woodruff," he explained, "to see the Price House, but we'll go back that way through Roebuck, where the Walnut Grove Plantation is located, and we'll swing through Spartanburg before we go home. Okay?"

"Sounds great," she told him. "You must know your way pretty well."

"I do," he agreed. "I've been there several times. I like history," he added with a grin.

It was a beautiful drive, through some of the prettiest country Maggie had ever seen, although it seemed to take a long time. But when they got to Woodruff, it wasn't quite time for the towering brick house to be open to the public, and they had to go to a nearby restaurant and drink coffee until eleven o'clock. When they got back, other tourists had gathered.

Bret paid the admission, refusing Maggie's offer of money, and then she forgot all about money as they toured the historic Price House. It had a steep gambrel roof and inside end chimneys, an acutely unique style for the Deep South. The bricks for the house with its flat face were made on the premises and laid in Flemish bond. It sat on what was once a two-thousand-acre plantation and was built in 1795—to serve as an inn as well as a home. Thomas Price, whose brainchild it was, also ran a post office and a general store. Period furniture graced the house, and Maggie felt the pull of the past strongly in its gracefully aging confines. The county historic preservation commission had obviously been active in the restoration.

When the tour was over, they climbed back into the car and headed north to Roebuck to tour Walnut Grove Plantation.

Maggie fell in love with the house, with its graceful front porch and chimneys at each end. It was clapboard over log construction with Queen Anne mantels and fielded paneling, and featured antique furnishings and accessories which portrayed living conditions in Spartanburg County before 1830.

The separate kitchen featured a collection of eighteenth-century utensils. There was a blacksmith's forge, a meat house, and a barn. And the office of the first doctor in the county.

All in all, it was fascinating. But Maggie found herself drawn to the grounds with their ancient oaks and walnuts, and the Moore family cemetery where Margaret Katherine Moore Barry was buried, along with other family members, slaves, and Revolutionary soldiers.

"She was a scout for General Morgan at the Battle of Cowpens," Bret remarked, nodding toward the grave, "and the daughter of the house."

"She must have been quite a lady," Maggie reflected, closing her eyes to drink in the delicious autumn air. "I wonder if she minds all these people tramping

137

through on floors that she swept with her own hands, and staring at her grave?"

"I doubt if she had to sweep floors," he murmured.

"I'm sure there were servants," she agreed. "But a woman brave enough to scout for the army would hardly be afraid to pick up a broom if she needed to. I'll bet she was something special," she added with a smile. "One of the first liberated women."

He laughed. "I've always thought that myself. The past is always with us, isn't it?" he mused, sticking his hands in his pockets to stare back at the house. "We're always curious about those who came before us. How they lived. How they survived. How they loved and hated, and how they died. The same as someday future historians will be curious about us, and our time."

She shivered delicately. "I don't like to think about that. We'll be dead."

He turned back. "What a profound thought. Are you afraid to die?"

She sighed. "Yes and no. I'm a good Presbyterian, you know, and I try to live my religion. But I'm not always as good as I wish I were," she added with a laugh.

"None of us is. I just live one day at a time, myself," he told her, "and do the best I can."

She smiled at him. "Which is all any of us can do, I suppose. The leaves are going," she added, nodding toward the partial bareness of some of the trees behind the house.

"We'd better be doing the same," he told her, checking his watch. "My gosh, I didn't realize it was so late. We're not going to have time for Cowpens today, I'm afraid. As it is, we'll be going home in the dark once we stop for supper."

"My fault," she said, apologizing. "I was so fascinated that I couldn't leave—"

"I enjoyed it," he said, cutting her off and grinning. "I like to see people appreciate history. Especially in my own state. Ready?"

"Whenever you are. It's been a great day," she added. "Thank you."

"Thank you," he returned. "We'll have to do this again."

She murmured something, not committing herself, because she was already dreading going back to the house. Saxon was going to be out for blood, and she knew it.

Lisa and Randy had gone out when Maggie said good night to Bret and walked into the silence of the house. But Sandra was still up, pacing the floor. She stopped at the sight of Maggie and went quickly out into the hall to meet her.

"Thank goodness you're home," she said with evident relief, a worried frown between her worried eyes. "Oh, Maggie, will you go up and see if Saxon will talk to you? He's locked himself in his room and hasn't eaten anything. . . . He won't let Randy in, he won't let me in—it's just so unlike him," she concluded helplessly. "Something must be wrong, and I'm so worried. Will you . . . ?"

"Of course," Maggie said gently, knowing what was wrong. It would have been amusing in other circumstances—a grown man throwing a tantrum because he hadn't got his own way. But as she

139

mounted the stairs she began to think about how very vulnerable his blindness made him. Sighted, he'd have forced her hand about Bret. They'd have fought it out verbally, or he might have come after her, but he'd never have locked himself away out of pique. He was blind, and it made him helpless in a new and frightening way. He couldn't deal with the world as he used to.

She sighed as she paused in front of his door before she knocked.

"Saxon?" she called gently.

There was no response. None at all.

She knocked again, louder. "Saxon!"

This time there was a muffled sound. "Go away!" His voice sounded strangely slurred.

"It's Maggie," she called again. "Please let me in!"

There was a long pause, during which she really worried. Then there was a thud and the sound of furniture and the door being knocked. A key turned. The door opened.

She gaped up at him, catching her breath. He was pale; his hair was tousled, his face unshaven. And he was standing there absolutely nude, without a stitch of clothing on his big, hair-roughened body.

CHAPTER TEN

Maggie gasped, but she couldn't drag her startled, fascinated eyes away. He was as appealing as a delicately carved Greek statue, not an ounce of flab or fat on him, all muscle and blatant masculinity.

"If you're coming in, come on," he growled, turning to weave his way back toward the bed.

She followed him, closing the door behind her, and watched him collapse into the rumpled brown sheets with a groan.

"You're ill," she burst out.

"I'm something," he said weakly. "Get me something cold to drink, will you, honey? God, I'm burning up!"

She had to steel herself to move closer, but she finally gathered enough courage to stand beside him and touch his broad forehead. It was blistering hot to the touch.

"Flu, I'll bet," she mumbled. "I'll be right back. And you should be under the covers."

"Then cover me up," he growled huskily. "God, it's hot. . . ."

He was rambling. She pulled the covers gently over him and went downstairs to tell Sandra, who in turn called the family doctor. He'd just arrived and gone upstairs when Lisa and Randy came in.

"What's going on?" Randy asked quickly.

"It's Saxon," Sandra said. "Maggie says he's burning with fever."

Randy shook his head. "Boy, that's one for the books," he remarked. "I can only remember half a dozen times I've ever seen him sick. How about some coffee while we wait for the verdict?"

"Maggie and I will make it," Lisa volunteered, leading her sister off into the kitchen.

"How bad is he?" Lisa asked as they filled the pot and made four strong cups of coffee.

"I don't know," Maggie mumbled. She put cups and saucers on a tray with cream and sugar. "I feel like it's my fault. He didn't want me to go out with Bret, and I did it for spite. . . ."

Lisa touched her arm gently. "It's probably just a virus. He'll be all right, really he will. He's so strong."

Tears misted the older woman's eyes, but she managed to smile through them. "I hope so."

Lisa hugged her. "Come on, let's go drink our coffee."

The doctor was back down in a few minutes, shaking his head. "Stubbornest man I ever knew," he grumbled, refusing Sandra's offer of coffee. "It's a virus, one of those forty-eight-hour things that I've seen a dozen cases of so far this week. I gave him an antibiotic and wrote a prescription for some tablets." He dug it out of his pocket and handed it to Sandra. "Give him those twice a day until they're all gone, keep him in bed, give him plenty of fluids, have him

142

take aspirin for the aching. If he isn't better in three days, call me."

"Thank you, Doctor Johnson," Sandra said gently. "I hated to ask you out at this hour of the night."

He grinned. "No trouble. It was a change from delivering babies; that's usually what I get called out at night for. Night."

"Good night."

Sandra escorted him out and started upstairs, leaving the rest of them to follow.

Saxon was under the covers, thank goodness, Maggie thought as they filed into his bedroom, but he looked like death, and he was still hot with fever.

"He needs sponging," Sandra remarked, wringing her hands nervously. "Randy . . ."

"Maggie," Saxon called huskily, holding out his hand. "The rest of you go watch television or something. I only need Maggie."

"But, darling . . ." Sandra protested gently.

Saxon's dark eyes opened threateningly, as intimidating without sight as they had been with it. "I said I want Maggie," he repeated hotly. "No one else!"

"We'd better humor him, Mother," Randy said with a wicked smile at Maggie. "He has good taste in nurses, after all."

"Are you sure you don't mind?" Sandra asked Maggie with a worried look.

"I don't mind at all," Maggie lied as she realized what staying with him was going to mean, and she still wasn't quite over the shock of seeing him au naturel.

"If you need us . . ." Lisa began.

"I'll scream and run up a flag, okay?" Maggie teased. "I've nursed you and Dad through flu and viruses; I know what to do. But I sure could use another cup of coffee."

"I'll bring you one," Lisa promised. She followed the others out the door and closed it behind her.

"My cold drink," Saxon added, reminding her.

"Oh, my gosh!" She ran to the door. "Lisa, will you bring Saxon a tall glass of something cold, please?" she called to her sister.

"Sure thing!" came the reply, drifting back up the staircase.

"Top reporter," Saxon chided when he heard her approach the bed. "Photographic memory."

"I was worried," she excused herself, reaching down to hold his big hand in her own. "Do you feel any better?"

"Why do people always think that having a needle stuck in their arms will improve their complaints?" he growled. "Now my arm hurts as well as the rest of me. Dan put the damned needle through the bone!"

"Shame on you," she chided gently. "Here he comes all the way out here in the middle of the night to see about you, and all you want to do is complain about the way he gives shots. I ought to call him up and tell him how ungrateful you are."

"You would, too, you little headache," he muttered, drawing in a hard breath. His eyes closed. "Maggie, I feel like hell. Don't leave me."

Her fingers tightened in his. "I won't. I won't."

He drank every drop of the iced soft drink that Lisa brought up with Maggie's coffee and then dozed off. But he woke again not two hours later, tossing and turning, and the fever was blazing.

The rest of the family had already gone to bed, but Maggie remembered what Sandra had said about sponging him down. It would certainly help to bring the fever back to normal while the antibiotic had time to work.

She got a basin and a soft sponge and, gritting her teeth, pulled back the covers and began to draw the damp sponge over his feverish body.

He stiffened at first at the unfamiliar touch, and then relaxed and lay back with a hard sigh, his eyes closed, his limbs barely stirring. She lingered over him, feeling his skin cool, watching the expressions that drifted over his broad, hard face. He needed her. For a few hours, he actually needed her.

She finished and drew the covers back over him, and he slept again. She sat beside him in an armchair, watching him, drinking in the sight of him, until the small hours of the morning. She could just barely keep her eyes open, and suddenly she couldn't keep them open at all. Her body slumped sideways in the chair and she slept.

He was still asleep when she woke and leaned forward to touch his face. It was cool, thank goodness; the fever had broken. She left him long enough to freshen up and change into a pair of brown jeans with a beige pullover top, and to get a tray to take back upstairs. Sandra had a meeting that morning with her church group, and Randy and Lisa were going downtown to start shopping for furniture for their new home.

"Do you mind if we all desert you?" Sandra asked

gently. "If he'd let us sit with him, I'd certainly do my share. . . ."

"I know that," Maggie said with a smile. "I don't mind, really."

"A labor of love, my dear?" Sandra asked in a tone soft with understanding.

Maggie, unembarrassed, nodded. "I'd better get this upstairs before he wakes," she said, indicating the tray. "I hope I can get him to eat something, even if it's just a piece of toast."

"Well," Randy remarked, "if he'll do it for anyone, it'll be for you."

"I hope you're right," she returned. "See you all later."

She fitted herself into the big armchair by his bed and nibbled at a piece of toast while she drank her coffee. He began to stir, his powerful legs flexing, and the covers went flying as he stretched.

"Maggie?" he murmured, turning his head toward the chair.

"I'm—I'm here," she managed, fighting to keep her eyes on his face.

One corner of his mouth turned up. "What color is your face?"

She cleared her throat. "How about some coffee and toast? I brought a pot and several buttered slices, and some jam."

He tugged the covers back up to his waist and sat up, propping back against the pillows. "I'd love the coffee, and one piece of toast, but without jam. I still feel a little weak. Have you been here all night?"

"Yes," she said, fixing his coffee and putting it within his reach, along with a piece of toast. She told him where it was and went back to her chair to watch him sip and nibble. "Randy's going to get your prescription filled and bring it back at lunchtime. The doctor said you didn't have to start them until tonight."

He finished his toast and swallowed his coffee. "I feel rusted," he remarked with a hard sigh. "Run me a tub of water, Maggie, and help me into it. And have the maid change these sheets, will you?"

"I'll change them," she said. "If you could wait until Randy gets home."

He lifted an eyebrow. "Embarrassed? There's nothing left that you haven't already seen. You're a big girl."

"Yes, I am, but—"

"Haven't you ever seen a man without his clothes before?"

"In books," she grumbled.

"Not in the flesh?" he teased. "My God, what a shock it must have been."

"Saxon, can't you wait until Randy gets back?" she asked.

He drew in a slow breath. "Maggie, I feel as if I haven't bathed for weeks, can you understand? I just want a tub of water. If you're too damned inhibited to help me, I'll manage alone."

"You make me sound like a prude," she grumbled. "All right, I'll help you. I don't suppose I could be any more shocked than I already am anyway."

"There's nothing shocking about nudity," he said. "Anyway God must not have thought so, because he made us originally without complete wardrobes."

"I suppose so," she admitted reluctantly. "But

people can make something disgusting out of it."

"Like pornography?" he asked. "Yes, I know. They take an act of love and make an act of degradation out of it. But between people who love each other, Maggie, it becomes an expression of something more than desire. Just as bodies become more than objects of depravity."

She got up, smoothing down her T-shirt. "I'm shy with you," she confessed. "It's something I can't help, I don't have the experience to pretend sophistication."

"I'm glad you haven't," he said quietly. "I don't want you to get that kind of experience with any man except me."

She cleared her throat. "I'll run the water."

His soft laughter followed her like a relentless wind.

When she'd filled the big tub and turned on the whirlpool, she arranged towels and washcloths and went back to get him, her heart in her throat.

He tossed aside the covers and stood up, unembarrassed even when she hesitated, and he must have known that she was looking at him.

"Care to get close enough to lend me your hand?" he teased.

"Of course." She took his fingers in hers and led him into the big blue-tiled bathroom. "Sorry, I was just reviewing an anatomy lesson," she added with a mischievous smile.

"Disappointed, Maggie?" he asked softly.

She lowered his hand to the side of the big tub. "I'll bet they absolutely swoon when you undress," she murmured.

148

"Why don't you climb in here with me?" he asked after a minute, his voice taut and coaxing all at once.

"Well . . ."

"It's a big tub," he remarked. "You couldn't have had time to bathe this morning. . . ."

Just the thought of being that close to him took her breath away, but she had just enough sanity left to refuse.

"I'll . . . have mine later," she breathed. "I—I had one before I left yesterday anyway."

"Coward," he accused silkily. He climbed into the tub and stretched out. "God, that feels good! Maggie, how about soaping my back, since you won't get in with me?"

She took the cloth and lathered it, sitting on the edge of the tub and trying not to feel the sensuous maleness of his muscular body as she drew it over his broad back and shoulders.

"Here," he murmured, drawing her hands around to his chest, leaning back with a contented sigh to let her soap it as well. Somewhere along the way, the cloth got lost, and her fingers were drawn to him like moths to a flame. Her breath caught; her heart seemed to be trying to climb up her throat as she explored the hard contours of his torso in a silence that blazed with excitement.

"Come in here with me," he breathed roughly. "I won't do anything you don't want me to do."

Her mind rebelled at the suggestion, even as her fingers were fumbling with her top and her jeans, and she was telling herself that this was insane, insane! But her body trembled with wanting, asserting itself for the first time in her life, demanding what it needed to survive.

She eased down into the warm water with him, feeling her skin slide against him, his powerful, hair-roughened thigh against her own, his arm reaching out to draw her close at his side.

"You see?" His voice was rough, ragged. "Maggie, you see?"

The words didn't make sense, but then they had nothing to do with what was happening, and they both knew it. Inevitably he turned, turning her with him so that her body was drawn fully against the length of his, and she felt the silken brush of flesh on flesh for the first time in the smooth warmth of the bathwater. Her legs entwined with his, trembling, her body tautened as her arms went around his shoulders and her breasts flattened against the soapy hair on his chest.

"Now," he groaned. His arms trembled as they drew her closer, and his mouth moved down to crush hers. The water swallowed them up to their necks, and under its churning surface she could feel his hands touching her as no man ever had before, exploring her, gentling her for what was surely to come.

"But . . . but we can't," she managed in a choked, half-whispered moan, trembling all over at the long sweet contact with his body.

"Why not?" he breathed, his tongue probing, darting past her teeth into the dark softness of her mouth, his hands gently lifting her hips and touching her thighs.

"Here?" she cried, but she was clinging, arching,

and all at once there was such a terrible urgency as she felt him move her, ease and surge against her, and her mouth bit into his, her nails wounded, her voice cried out wildly in the sudden silence as the world darkened and reddened and spun away in a shimmer of fiery explosions around her and pain became a kind of terrible sweet necessity. . . .

Maggie had always heard that men lost interest once their appetites were satisfied, but Saxon held her and brushed soft, tender kisses all over her face until she was calm once more. His fingers moved against her cheeks, her mouth, her neck, and he murmured things she barely heard at all, her body still racked by the aftermath of a pleasure that defied description.

"I thought . . . it was supposed to hurt," she murmured into his shoulder, feeling a little chill, as the water was just barely lukewarm.

"It did," he murmured at her ear. "You just didn't care," he added with a smile in his voice.

She drew back a little, embarrassed. "It's so strange, that you can want, *need,* pain in small doses. Why?"

"I don't know either, darling," he confessed quietly. "I only know that in all my life, there's never been anything like this, with anyone. I'm only just beginning to understand why the French call lovemaking 'the little death.' "

"It was that, wasn't it?" she breathed, leaning forward to brush her mouth softly against his, loving the hard warmth of it, loving the feel of his body next to hers.

He drew in a deep breath, his hands going to her

shoulders, an odd kind of concern in his scowling expression. "Maggie, we'd better get out of here. The water's going cold."

"Oh, yes—yes, of course," she stammered. She struggled out, grabbing up a towel to wrap around herself and handing a larger one to him. They dried themselves in a stiff silence, and she walked back in the bedroom ahead of him to get a pair of pajama bottoms. She handed them to him and turned away to dress herself. When he finished, she led him back to his bed.

"I'll dry your hair, if you like," she volunteered in a dull tone.

"No," he sighed. "It's all right, I've gotten most of the water out of it. You'd better dry your own."

"I—I'll do that." She searched for something to say, but she was oddly shy with him now; she felt nervous, uncertain. He seemed to regret what had happened, and she turned away, still trying to reconcile her body's demanding hunger with her own reticence. She hadn't believed people could lose control of themselves so easily, so completely. Now it had happened, and the thought suddenly occurred to her that she could be pregnant. She hadn't even thought about the consequences—not once! All her upbringing, all her principles, had fallen to the wayside because of her unquenchable desire for a man who'd wanted nothing more than a body. And now he was regretting it, and so was she, but it was too late.

She dried her hair and spent several minutes in her room, trying to compose herself enough to go back. But the longer she waited, the more impossible it seemed. How could she face him after that wild abandon? *In the bathtub!* How could she ever face him again? Her eyes closed. Her body was already beginning to feel bruised from the porcelain. They must have been out of their minds!

Well, at least Saxon knew now that he was still a man, despite his blindness, she thought bitterly. And since he had what he'd wanted from her since she came back here, he probably wouldn't want her again. Had it been desire? Or had he been jealous of Bret—so jealous that he felt he had to assert his mastery over her? Or were there deeper, darker reasons? Was it revenge for what that misplaced by-line had caused, revenge for the blindness that his subconscious blamed her for causing?

The thought paralyzed her. At the time she'd thought it was out of love. She'd convinced herself that the endearments he'd whispered, the ardent commands that led her into the sweet wildness of emotion, had been purely out of love. But now she had doubts. Couldn't any woman have pleased him, despite what he'd said? Couldn't he have attained that pleasure with anyone? After all, Maggie thought, men were structured to enjoy sex regardless of their partners—weren't they?

The longer she hesitated, the bigger the doubts grew, until she convinced herself that what had happened was nothing more than a sordid excursion into animal pleasure, a mistake that never should have happened.

She moved out into the hall just as Randy came down it.

"Randy, would you change the sheets for Saxon?"

she asked hurriedly. "I've got to go out for a few minutes . . ."

"Oh, sure," he agreed with a pleasant smile. "Did you get any rest?"

"I slept a little, I just need some fresh air, that's all," she assured him. "Thanks a million."

She darted down the staircase, grateful that there was no one in sight, because she was crying.

She wandered around out on the grounds for hours, brooding, hating herself, hating Saxon. There was only one thing to do. Go home. Now. Before, out of some horrible circumstance, she wound up in his arms again. Once could be excused on the grounds of temporary insanity, but twice would be unforgiveable.

She wrapped her arms around her, feeling the cold as never before. She went back into the house and up the staircase, feeling like a prisoner going to the guillotine.

She knocked at Saxon's door, jumping when she heard the harsh "Come in!"

She opened the door and moved hesitantly into the room. He was under the sheets, smoking a cigarette, his face dark and lined heavily.

"Who is it?" he asked.

"Maggie," she said hesitantly.

A remarkably elated expression crossed his broad face; his eyes seemed to kindle as they turned toward the sound of her voice.

"Maggie!" he breathed. He held out his free hand. "Honey, come here."

She moved closer, but she wouldn't take the out-

154

stretched hand. She avoided it as if it were a red-hot poker.

"I've—I've been thinking," she said.

"So have I," he admitted, reluctantly drawing his hand back to clench it on the covers. "Maggie, we'd better get married."

Of all the things she'd expected him to say, that was the last, the very last. She stood gaping at him as if he'd offered to eat one of the curtains at the window.

"Why?" she blurted out.

He took a draw from the cigarette, looking impatient and terribly irritated. "Because you could be pregnant," he said bluntly. "Or hasn't that occurred to you? I was too far gone to think about protecting you."

She caught her breath. "That's not the best reason to get married," she said quietly, forcing her voice to be calm, to deny what she wanted most in all the world—to be Saxon's wife.

"What would be a good one then?" he asked harshly.

"Love," she returned. "On both sides, Saxon, not just one."

He seemed to freeze, to become rigid. His hand on the bed clenched until the knuckles were white, but her eyes were on his face and she didn't see them.

"You don't think love could come naturally?" he asked after a minute.

"I think we'd be crazy to take such a chance," she said sadly. Her eyes closed.

"And then, too, I'm blind," he ground out. "Not the greatest prospective husband in the world."

"That has nothing to do with it!" she protested. "Saxon, if you had your sight, none of this would even have happened, don't you realize that? You wouldn't have been jealous enough of Bret to seduce me, or so hungry for a woman that you lost your head. You wouldn't have—have wanted me!" Her voice broke, and with a tiny cry she whirled and ran for the door.

"Maggie, you crazy little fool!" he burst out. "Maggie!"

But she didn't stop, couldn't stop. He didn't love her. It was only guilt that made him suggest marriage, because he thought she might be pregnant. She couldn't let him trap himself into a marriage he didn't want. Without love it would never be enough. And if he fell in love with someone else, and found himself tied to her, it would have been more than she could bear.

She ran down the stairs, her eyes blinded by tears, vaguely aware of footsteps behind her. She stopped on the bottom step as she heard Saxon calling her.

She looked up to see him on the top step, his hand clutching at the banister.

"Saxon, no!" she screamed as his hand missed. "No!"

But the warning came too late. He went headfirst down the stairs with a horrible thud, tossing and pitching. She rushed toward him, but she wasn't in time to break the fall. She felt her own head knock against a step as she helped to stop his descent, but she held on, praying that it would be enough to spare him more pain.

They came to a tumbled heap at the bottom of the

steps, sprawled over each other. She dragged herself up and looked at him. He was unconscious; his eyes were closed, his face white and devoid of expression, and there was blood at his right temple.

CHAPTER ELEVEN

The next few hours went by in a blur. Maggie must have screamed because when she looked up, Randy and Sandra were bending over Saxon, and Lisa was holding her close to keep her from throwing herself on Saxon's unconscious body.

She could barely tell them what had happened, her voice incoherent through tears, her eyes riveted to Saxon, her hand clinging to his until the arrival of the ambulance, which seemed to have taken an eternity. She rode with him in it, never leaving his side until they took him into the emergency room.

Finally Dr. Johnson came out to speak to the family, with a long technical description of what had happened.

"The most important thing," he concluded, holding Sandra's trembling hands tightly as the others gathered around him, "is that, because of the fall, the shrapnel has shifted. It's still not operable, but—with any luck at all, my dear—when Saxon recovers, he'll be able to see again."

Sandra caught her breath, and Maggie's face lighted up. He might be able to see! If that happened, perhaps he could even forgive her for this, for putting him in the hospital. . . .

Tears rolled down Maggie's cheeks. If only. If only! She wouldn't mind giving him up if it would mean having him sighted again. She wouldn't mind losing him forever, as long as he could feel whole again. It would be worth anything!

Sandra turned toward her when the doctor had gone, promising to advise them of every new development.

"You see?" she whispered tearfully, holding Maggie close for an instant. "Everything always works out for the best. You were blaming yourself, my dear, but if he hadn't taken that fall . . . he may see again! He may see again."

Randy reached out a brotherly hand and ruffled Maggie's hair. "Will you calm down now?" He grinned. "It's going to be fine. Honest it is."

Lisa added her own enthusiasm to Randy's, gathering Maggie to her side. They stayed all through the long day until Saxon was finally conscious and able to receive visitors. They had to go in one at a time, so Maggie let the others go first—not so much out of consideration as pure cowardice. Finally it was her turn.

Maggie had never been as nervous as when she paused at the door of his room. She was wearing a simple green shirtwaist dress in a soft wool blend, beige boots, and her hair was soft and freshly washed and curling around her face. It had grown a little, but it would take a long time for it to grow as long as it had been when she first met Saxon, Maggie thought.

She wondered how long it would take his thick hair to grow out again.

She pushed open the door and went in, surprised to find him sitting up in bed. The room, Maggie noticed, was dimly lighted.

He turned when she walked in, and his pupils seemed to dilate as they looked at her. They traced every line of her face before they fell to her body, lingering lovingly on every soft curve of it. He smiled faintly, his face mirroring masculine appreciation.

"Several days too late to do me much good," he murmured enigmatically, and caught her eyes just as the statement made blatant sense in her whirling mind.

She colored, and he saw it and laughed gently.

"Come in and sit down," he said.

She moved to the chair by the bed and sat on its edge, her purse held tensely on her lap.

"How—how are you?" she asked hesitantly. "How do you feel?"

"Sore," he murmured with a wry smile. "Tough as nails. Delighted. Able to conquer the world. A lot of things. Maggie, how do you feel?"

"Guilty," she replied without thinking, and her eyelids flinched as she looked at him. "Saxon, I'm so sorry!"

"For what?" he burst out. "For making it possible for me to see again? You crazy woman!"

"For making you fall down the staircase!" she corrected. "You could have broken your neck!"

"But I didn't. And it was worth it." His eyes searched hers and narrowed. "You were wrong, you know," he added quietly. "You don't seem to believe what I say, but it was you I wanted that morning, no one else."

She dropped her eyes. "Please, let's not talk about it. I only want to forget."

There was a potent silence before he spoke. "Was it that bad?" he ground out.

She swallowed. "How long will you have to be in the hospital?" she asked.

"Stop hedging," he said, watching her. "I want you to tell me. Was it that bad?"

She looked up, and the memory of lying in his big arms lighted a candle inside her, making her face glow with remembered pleasure. "No," she admitted.

With a long sigh he leaned back against the pillows, and his eyes closed for an instant. "I can see a distinct advantage in being sighted with you," he muttered. "You can hide things from me if all I have to go by is your voice."

She stared at the purse in her lap. "How does it feel—to be able to see?"

"There aren't words enough," he said simply. "We take sight for granted, you know, until we don't have it anymore. A simple thing like staring at the ceiling takes on mammoth proportions." He smiled faintly. "I'll never take it for granted again, I promise you."

"What will you do now?" she asked gently.

He shrugged. "When they let me out of here, I'll go back to work," he said. His head turned and he stared at her through narrowed eyes. "Still feeling guilty, or are you just wondering whether or not I'll be willing to part with your 'services' now that I can see again?"

161

It was like a slap in the face. *Services*—as if she were a common prostitute. She stiffened, but years of reporting had taught her to conceal her deepest emotions behind a mask, and she did it now.

She laughed shortly. "You'll hardly need me, with all those very eligible beauties vying for your attention, will you?"

"Missing your job?" he said, taunting.

She shrugged. "I always have," she said with a cool smile. "I haven't found anything yet that could replace it."

"Not even in that tub with me?" he asked abruptly, and studied her delicately flushing face with eyes that missed nothing. "You might be interested to know that, of all the places I've had encounters with women, that was a first."

She tried to look sophisticated and failed miserably. "Oh, don't," she managed, turning her face away.

"You little prude," he scoffed, his voice deep and faintly amused. "Did you blush all over when you looked at me?"

She drew in a shuddering breath. "Yes, I did," she admitted. "Are you enjoying yourself, Saxon? Would you like to stick pins in me too?"

He studied her for a long time, dissecting the emotions chasing each other across her averted face. "I wasn't kidding when I asked you to marry me," he said out of the blue. "We both know that you could be pregnant."

She nodded, her eyes on her hands. "I could be. But there's just as much chance that I'm not. I still think it's crazy to get married without . . . without being sure."

He sighed, his eyes closing. "Maybe you're right," he said in a weary tone. "Maybe it is crazy. But, Maggie, I'm forty years old. You're—what? Twenty-six? How much longer have both of us got to go looking for a mate? We're compatible—we're damned compatible physically. Could you do better, all conceit aside? I can give you most any material thing you want. I'll . . . I'll take care of you, Maggie," he added, and she felt the hesitation; it was as if he'd meant to say something quite different but had thought better of it.

She felt like getting up and running. It wasn't something she should even consider. Despite the risk of pregnancy, it was crazy to let herself be coerced into a marriage like this, when she knew that he didn't love her—not in the way a man should love a woman to consider marrying her. Marriage was so permanent!

She looked up at him with all her uncertainties in her wide eyes. "What if you fall in love with someone else?" she asked quietly. "What if—what if I do?" she added, knowing the chances were billions to one, but too insecure to admit that she loved him and to risk rejection.

He flexed his shoulders. "We'll cross that bridge when we come to it. Well?" His dark eyes bored into hers, and one heavy eyebrow arched up toward the bandage around his head. "Still doubting? Come here, Maggie, and I'll convince you in the best possible way."

She really should have left while she was ahead,

she told herself. But she wanted him so, loved him so. Her mind was overruled by her rebellious heart. She got up out of the chair, aware of the faint shock in his expression when she went unresisting to him and sat gently on the edge of the bed.

"Are you sure you're up to it?" she asked quietly, searching his drawn face.

"With you?" he asked in a deep, hushed tone. "My God, don't you know that I could get off my deathbed to make love to you? Come down here. . . ."

His hand caught her upper arm and jerked her down against his broad chest. His mouth found hers in one smooth motion, his lips probing and demanding, his tongue invading her yielded mouth.

His fingers caught in her short hair and thrust her face hard against his, urgency in the sudden pressure of his mouth.

"No," she whispered shakily.

His nostrils flared as he let her draw away, but his eyes promised retribution. "I want you," he ground out, holding her gaze relentlessly. "Any way I can get you. And you want me. Won't that do, Maggie? Do you have to have promises of undying love as well?"

She touched his broad face with fingers that adored it, testing the texture of his cheeks, his lips. "No," she sighed miserably, "I suppose not." Her eyes searched his quietly. "At least I'm walking in with my eyes wide open, so to speak. I won't be expecting a saint."

"That's a good thing," he said, "because you won't be getting one. God knows, I'm not perfect."

Her lips pursed in faint mischief. "Oh, maybe in one respect . . ." she murmured suggestively.

He caught his breath and drew her fingers to his mouth, nibbling at them with his lips, his teeth. "Did you like it?" he whispered sensuously.

Her breath began to catch in her throat. "Yes," she admitted.

"Next time," he whispered huskily, holding her eyes, "it's going to be in a bed, with the lights blazing. Or in broad daylight so that I can see you, really see you, while we make love."

Her body tingled wildly, her heart ran away. "Saxon, would you want to have a baby?" she asked in a stranger's voice.

"Oh, God. . . ." He groaned, dragging her mouth down to his. He kissed her wildly, roughly, his mouth frankly hurting in his sudden ardor. "Of course, I'd want to have a baby," he ground out, his voice shaking, his hand trembling as it held her mouth down to his.

"A little boy with dark eyes and big hands," she breathed into his open mouth.

"A little girl with green eyes and long legs," he corrected, biting at her lips, his breath ragged.

"One of each," she promised as he kissed her again, letting her feel the soft, slow pressure in every aching line of her lips before he increased it.

Neither of them heard the door open or the nurse's aide's discreet clearing of her throat until she did it loudly for the second time.

Maggie drew back, red-faced. "Oh!" she cried. "Uh, do you need me to—to step out into the hall?"

The older woman, a redhead, was grinning. "Only

if you need the exercise," she said. "I knew he was dangerous the minute I laid eyes on him in the hall."

He grinned at her. "Well, there isn't a lot to do in here," he remarked. "I had to import my own toy. . . ."

The older woman laughed, winking at Maggie. "Listen to him! Don't you let him corrupt you, my dear. I know his type!"

"You're too late," Saxon informed her. "She just agreed to marry me."

"Poor thing," the nurse sighed, patting Maggie on the shoulder. "You make him treat you right, now, you hear? I'll just fill up your ice jug, Mr. Tremayne. Would you like some juice?"

"No, but I'd love a cup of coffee, if it's possible," he said with a smile that could have charmed a charging cow.

"I'll get you one," the aide said. "For you too?" she added, lifting her brows at Maggie.

"I'd love one," came the smiling reply.

"Back in a jiffy," the aide called over her shoulder.

Saxon grinned up at her, his face relaxed, his eyes soft and dark. There was something different about him but something vaguely familiar in the look. . . .

"Don't think so hard; you'll hurt yourself," he murmured. He touched her cheek with the backs of his fingers, his eyes sketching every line of her face. "When?" he asked.

"When what?" she murmured.

"When will you marry me? Suppose we make it a double wedding with Lisa and Randy. Would you mind?" he asked.

She caught her breath. "It's barely six weeks away. . . ."

He put his finger over her lips, and his eyes were solemn. "I can wait six weeks—just. If you put me off any longer than that, quite frankly you aren't going to be able to keep me out of your bed. I want you desperately."

She drew in a steadying breath, melting under the fierce hot gaze. "All right," she agreed hesitantly. "Six weeks."

His chest rose and fell heavily. "Get me out of this place," he said curtly. "Bake me a cake with a file in it or something."

She laughed. "I'll smuggle in a helicopter at the first opportunity," she promised, and didn't resist when he pulled her back down and kissed her again.

The rest of the family was delighted when they heard the news. Lisa wept with her sister, and Sandra immediately started adding to the Christmas wedding plans by ordering another batch of invitations for Saxon and Maggie. Randy, grinning, remarked that his stepbrother was finally getting some good sense in his old age, but that it was too bad that it had taken blindness and a fall down the staircase to get him to the altar.

Maggie spent her days with Saxon as he continued his recuperation at home. She had accepted the true nature of the wedding, knowing that he didn't love her, but too hungry for him to refuse. At least he wanted her. And perhaps when children came along, he'd learn to love her. She had to keep believing that; it was the only thing that made it bearable. And

167

meanwhile she delighted in Saxon's company and the caresses that were becoming so deliciously familiar.

"What about your book?" she asked him a few days after he came home, when they were sitting in his study with the door closed while a cheery fire burned in the fireplace.

"The book?" He smiled. "Well, I might finish it someday. But since I don't need it to keep you here . . ."

"I wouldn't have left you," she admitted, curled up on the sofa with her feet tucked under her jeaned legs under the blue T-shirt. "It was nice to be needed."

He turned from the fireplace. "I still need you," he said quietly.

"Do you?" She stared down at her legs in the faded jeans.

He moved back toward her and sat down beside her. "I haven't made love to you since I've been home," he said gently, "because I wasn't sure that I could stop."

Her eyes darted up to his, and she caught her breath. "Oh," she said.

He smiled faintly. "Were you worried?"

She lifted her shoulders. "I'm not sure. I—well, I wondered if you were having second thoughts, that's all."

He caught her hand and held its soft palm to his mouth. "No, honey, I'm not having second thoughts. Are you?"

She smiled up at him. "No."

His eyes dropped to the low neckline of her T-shirt and darkened perceptibly. For several seconds his breath seemed to roughen before he let go of her hand and turned away to lean back against the sofa beside her and close his eyes.

"It's getting late," he said after a minute. "You'd better get some sleep."

Disappointed, she sighed deeply and started to get up.

He caught her shoulder as she started to rise and turned her, searching her face. "Maggie . . ." he whispered unsteadily.

Helplessly, she dropped down into his lap, her arms looping behind his head to tug it down. "Kiss me," she whispered shakily. "Oh, Saxon, kiss me very hard!"

His mouth crushed down against hers, and they kissed as if it had been weeks instead of days. She felt the rapidness of his heartbeat, like that of her own, drowning in the pleasure of being close to him, kissed by him, wanted by him. It had been far too long already.

She felt him shift, so that they were lying side by side, and one big warm hand slid under the T-shirt to rest against her waist.

"Is that all you're going to do?" she whispered under his mouth.

"What do you want me to do?" he asked with a wicked smile as he propped himself up on an elbow to study her.

"I thought I was the one who needed teaching," she murmured dryly.

"In this," he said, letting his fingers move slowly up her rib cage, his eyes holding hers, "we're both beginners, Maggie."

"Beginners?" she breathed.

"Uh-huh," he murmured. His fingers easily disposed of the clasp of her bra, moving up to find the satin skin that firmed under his light touch. "Is this what you wanted?" he asked.

"Almost," she admitted, her breath catching as she responded unashamedly to the sensations he was causing.

His eyebrow jerked, and he smiled mischievously. "Then how about this, little one?" he murmured, slowly teasing the hem of the T-shirt up her body, exposing first her waist, then her ribs, and finally the soft curves of her breasts. And there he froze, the smile vanishing as he looked at her for the first time, seeing the vibrant flesh that he'd only touched before.

"Are you . . . are you disappointed?" she asked hesitantly when he didn't move.

His breath sighed out through taut lips. His eyes moved back up to hers. "No, I'm not disappointed," he said in a deep, husky tone. He bent again, and she watched his mouth open as it caught the taut peak between his lips and found it with his tongue. She arched helplessly, her hands holding him to her, her breath trapped in her throat as the magic began working on her.

His fingers bit into her, hurting, as his mouth grew more demanding. With a harsh sound he moved back to her mouth, poising just above it, his eyes fierce as they looked down into hers.

"Maggie—" he bit off. His hands took her body as his mouth took her parted lips, and she sank into the soft cushions under his formidable weight, accepting it joyously, without a semblance of protest.

She stretched under him, sensuously, feeling the powerful muscles of his legs brushing against hers in the silence that lengthened between them, punctuated by the sounds of harsh breathing and material brushing material, with the angry hiss of the fire close by. . . .

His shirt was off, his bareness touching hers, when he drew back, his body shuddering with the effort of stopping. He rested his forehead against hers and fought to catch his breath.

"Oh, baby, you go to my head like bourbon," he murmured roughly.

She touched his broad shoulders gently, feeling the taut muscles contract.

"You're so strong," she whispered shakily.

"And you're very soft," he whispered back, his lips smiling as they touched hers. "Want me?"

"Yes," she said honestly. Her fingers brushed against his mouth. "Saxon . . ."

He shook his head. "Not tonight." He kissed her once more and sat up, refastening her bra, tugging her shirt back in place with slightly unsteady fingers.

"Why?" she asked softly.

He drew her into a sitting position and brushed a kiss against her forehead. "Because what happened in my bathroom was an accident—something I never meant to happen. The next time we make love, it won't be on the spur of the moment or because I happened to lose my head. It's going to be because we both want it, and with my ring on your finger."

"You really didn't mean it to happen?" she asked quietly, curious.

He let her go long enough to light a cigarette, and drew her beside him as he leaned back to smoke it. "No," he admitted. "At first I was teasing. Then, when I felt you against me, I lost sight of everything except how much I needed you. And from there, my darling," he laughed gently, "it was all downhill. I couldn't even manage to get you out of the tub first; I couldn't wait."

"Neither could I," she admitted on a sigh. "It was so beautiful, even like that. . . . I hadn't realized that people could go so crazy all at once. I wasn't even thinking, I was only feeling, and it was so delicious that I couldn't stop."

"It's always going to be like that," he told her. "As long as we live."

She looked up at him with quiet, adoring eyes. Yes, she thought, they'd always be good together in bed. But how would they survive without love? Would her love for him be strong enough to keep the marriage together? Perhaps when there were children. . . .

"Get Sandra to go shopping with you tomorrow and find a wedding gown," he said suddenly.

"I suppose I'd better," she sighed, nestling closer. "It isn't that far away. I thought something beige. . . ."

"White," he corrected shortly, tilting her face up to his darkening eyes. "You came to me a virgin. White, Maggie."

Her lips parted on an intake of breath as she looked up at him.

"As far as I'm concerned," he said softly, "the marriage ceremony is a formality after the fact. When I took you, that was the beginning. I feel just as wed to you right now as I will when we put our signatures to the license and I place the ring on your finger." He took her left hand in his and kissed it. "What kind of ring would you like? A diamond?"

"I'd like an emerald," she replied. "A small one, set in white gold, with a band to match. How about you?"

He smiled. "You want me to wear a band?"

"Well, if you don't want to, I don't mind." She was lying, and avoided his gaze. "Some men would rather not, I know."

"Do you want me to?"

She shifted restlessly. "It's up to—"

"I said," he whispered, making her look at him, "do *you* want me to?"

She drew in a slow breath. "Yes," she admitted, throwing caution to the winds. "Yes, I do, I want those swooning women to know that you belong to me."

His fingers spread out against her throat, easing her head back on his shoulder while something dark and wild kindled in the eyes looking down into hers. "Say that again. . . ."

"What?"

"That I'm going to belong to you," he murmured.

She flushed and tried to hide her eyes, but he wouldn't let her. "You'll . . . belong to me," she managed as his penetrating gaze made her knees feel weak.

173

"And you'll belong to me," he whispered back. "Body and heart and soul?"

"Body and heart and soul," she breathed. Her fingers reached up hesitantly to touch his face, his broad forehead, his eyebrows, his nose, his mouth. "All of me."

"Do you know the words of the marriage ceremony?" he asked against her forehead.

"Love, honor, and cherish . . ."

"And with my body I thee worship," he whispered fervently. His hands brought her against him, and he folded her into his body, his big arms swallowing her against his still bare chest, so that her hands were crushed into the thick mat of hair over the warm muscles. "Did I please you that morning?" he asked huskily. "Did I give you the kind of pleasure I meant to?"

"Yes," she whispered, clinging. "Oh, yes, Saxon. You gave me pleasure."

"And if there wasn't the possibility of a child," he continued quietly, "if I hadn't lost my head . . . would you still be marrying me at Christmas?"

She hesitated. He was asking her to make an admission that she was afraid to make. She could bear loving him in silence, but could she bear his pity if he knew the truth? She hesitated, frozen against his warm body.

He tipped her chin up, watching her quietly, intently. "I need to know," he said. "I have to know. Am I blackmailing you into a relationship you don't want?"

"I—I want you very much," she said.

"I know that. But it isn't what I asked." He

pushed the wild hair away from her cheeks, her temples. "Maggie, I can force it out of you. You know that, don't you? All I have to do is strip you and start touching you. You'll tell me anything then, won't you?"

She swallowed. "Probably," she admitted. "But I'd despise you."

"Then don't goad me into it. Answer me."

Her eyes closed. "Are you going to strip me of pride too?"

"There isn't much room for pride in a good marriage," he reminded her. "Marriage is a compromise. It takes two people and an equal amount of give and take on both sides. Come on, Maggie, tell me. If you weren't afraid that I'd made you pregnant, would you still marry me?"

"Would you want to marry me if you weren't concerned about the possibility of a child?" she threw back.

He bent and touched her mouth very gently with his. "I would want you," he said in a deep, harsh tone, "if you were barren forever. I would want you if you were blind and deaf and helpless." His arms tightened. "I want children with you, but they don't have anything to do with the reasons I want to marry you."

She caught her breath at the tone of his voice. Her fingers speared into the hair over his broad chest and tangled there, pressing and pulling sensuously as the words began to penetrate her mind.

"Why do you want to marry me?" she asked.

"I asked you first."

She reached up and pressed her lips softly, warmly

to his, opening them to coax his mouth into following suit. Her tongue traced the thin upper lip, the slightly fuller lower one, and his hands dug in at her waist under the tormenting pressure.

"What are you doing, you little witch?" he growled huskily.

"I'm showing you why I want to marry you," she murmured impishly. "I adore you. I love your body. I love your eyes and your nose and this little frown between your eyes. I love the way you look without clothes and the way you kiss. . . ."

"Say the words, Maggie," he ground out. "Oh, God, say the words. . . . I need them so!"

"I love you, Saxon," she breathed into his mouth, feeling with wonder the tremor that ran through his big body, the surge of possession in the arms that swallowed her completely. "I love you until I ache with it."

"Baby," he breathed, bending. His mouth opened against hers, fitting itself exactly to the bow of her parted lips, taking slow, sweet possession of them.

She felt him move, laying her down on the couch, his body following hers, melting down over it as they kissed slowly, tenderly, in a way they never had before.

"You only call me baby . . . when we make love," she whispered against his mouth.

"I can find other words, if you want me to," he whispered back. "Darling, honey, my heart, my own . . . my love."

"I—I like that last one," she murmured.

His nose rubbed against hers. "Do you want to hear it too?" he whispered. "That I love you?"

"Do you?" she breathed, barely able to breathe as she looked up at him, waiting, hoping against hope, needing.

"Hopelessly," he admitted softly, searching her eyes as everything he felt began to glow in his own. "Helplessly. Like a boy of fifteen. Since the day I opened my office door and found you standing outside almost a year ago."

"Oh, Saxon," she ground out, closing her eyes as she pressed against him, hiding her face in his throat.

"I haven't had a woman since that day," he whispered into her ear. "Not until that morning in the tub. I didn't even try, Maggie; there was nobody for me but you. Nobody. I've loved you for so long. . . ."

"And I've loved you." She groaned. "I went through the motions of living, but all the while I thought you were hating me. And when I found out that you were Randy's stepbrother, I was convinced that you'd gotten me here for revenge."

"When I found out that Lisa was your sister, I went crazy trying to think of ways to get you here," he confessed, holding her closer. "When I finally got Randy to think of asking you up here with Lisa for a visit, it was all I could do to sound indifferent. But I encouraged him every step of the way. I wanted you with me until I could taste it. And then, pretending to want revenge was the only way I could think of to keep you. Blackmail, intimidation, guilt . . . my God, the underhanded things I've done to stop you from leaving me!"

"Seducing me," she added with a sigh.

"I didn't plan that," he said, laughing. "But it

seemed so completely natural at the time, so right. You were my first virgin, did you know?"

She shifted, drawing back to look up at him with smiling eyes. "I don't know whether to be jealous of all those women you got your experience with, or grateful to them. You made it so incredibly good for me."

"It was the same for me," he said, smoothing back her hair. "I'd never made love to a woman I was in love with, until then." He laughed softly. "I could have protected you, but I didn't. I wanted the threat of a child, I wanted a child with you. So I thought, What the hell, and just went ahead. I hoped that the risk might coerce you into saying yes when I asked you to marry me. And it did."

She shook her head. "No, it didn't," she corrected. "If I hadn't loved you, I'd have said no in spite of that risk. But you were offering me paradise. How could I have refused?"

His big hand went to her stomach, flattening out on it possessively. "Will you mind being pregnant so soon?" he asked gently.

"We aren't sure yet," she reminded him.

He brushed her mouth with his. "I'm afraid that by Christmas we will be," he whispered sensuously, moving against her so that she was made blatantly aware of his hunger. "I could stay away when I wasn't sure of you. But now that I am, I want you more than ever. And you already know that I'm not going to take no for an answer, don't you?"

Her breath caught in her throat as he eased her shirt back up, and began to remove it. "The door . . ."

"I locked it when we came in here," he murmured against her parted lips. "Relax, darling. This time it's going to be everything either one of us could want. It's no spur-of-the-moment thing, no impulse. You're going to be mine for the rest of our lives."

While he was whispering, her shirt was being gently pulled over her head, leaving her bare from the waist up. He looked down at her with frankly worshiping eyes, learning every line of her, every curve in the static silence that followed.

"The lights . . ." she protested, flushing at the intensity of his gaze.

"Do you remember that I once told you I'd never made love in the dark?" he murmured, bending to brush his mouth slowly, agonizingly against the soft slow sweep of her breasts.

Her hands tangled in his hair, and she caught her breath at the new sensations, the slowness that hadn't been possible that wild morning.

"And I'd never made love at all," she whispered.

"And I couldn't wait," he recalled with faint amusement. "I was so hungry for you, so much in love with you. I used to lie awake thinking about how it would be, how I'd draw it out and make it so sweet for you the first time. . . ."

She nuzzled against him, loving the thickness of his hair against her chin as he traced patterns on her bareness with his lips, his tongue. Her body lifted invitingly.

"It was sweet," she whispered. "Even though I had bruises all over."

"So did I," he murmured. "Help me. Here."

He moved her fingers to his belt and watched her flush and fumble with wicked eyes.

"On the sofa?" she whispered unsteadily.

"It's softer than the floor," he observed. "Unless . . ." He glanced toward the thick rug in front of the fireplace and cocked an eyebrow suggestively. "Well?"

The thought of that softness under her bare skin made her tingle all over. She caught her breath, and he read the answer in her eyes. He got up, shedding the rest of his clothes before he eased her out of her own and carried her to the rug.

She sank down into it, moving sensuously as she felt the furry thickness surround her, and watched him as he moved to poke up the fire in the fireplace before he came to her.

He smiled, half amused at the open curiosity in her gaze, the pleasure revealed in her misty eyes.

"Another first?" he murmured as he eased down beside her to prop himself up on an elbow, his body touching hers gently, making her want more than the light contact. "I gather that nude men weren't on your list of familiar things."

"I thought I mentioned that once before," she murmured. "Oh, Saxon, you have to be the most magnificent man . . ."

"You could pass for a particularly lovely Greek statue yourself," he replied, looking at her long slender body with a lover's eyes. "Maggie," he breathed, lifting his hand to run it slowly, lingeringly, down every soft inch of her, "I want you more than I can find words to tell you about it. I want to grow old with you. I want your children to be mine. I want to spend the rest of my life loving you, cherishing you . . ."

"I feel the same way about you," she replied. Her legs moved as she pressed her body softly against his, smiling at his involuntary response, the sudden tautness under the warmth of powerful muscle. "Make it last . . . a long time," she whispered softly, lifting her hands to tangle and tug gently at the mat of hair over his chest. "Make it last forever this time."

His breath came harshly, jerkily. One powerful leg insinuated itself across both of hers, and his hand flattened on her belly before it began to move in new, unfamiliar ways on her body.

She cried out involuntarily, trembling, her wide, awed eyes meeting his as her nails bit into him.

He smiled slowly, triumphantly. "Suppose I tell you exactly what I'm going to do to you," he whispered, bending to nip at her mouth with a slow, teasing pressure. "And how I'm going to do it," he added, laughing softly when she arched and moaned wildly. "Oh, yes, darling, it's good, isn't it? And this is just the beginning, just the tip of the iceberg."

"Saxon," she bit off, her hands clinging, pulling, her eyes pleading, her body on fire from head to toe as he teased and tormented. "I love you, I love you!"

"I love you," he whispered back. "I love every inch of you, every curve, every line. With my body I thee worship. This is where our marriage begins, here, now, as surely as if the marriage contract were already signed, the rings in place, the vows spoken. You're mine, and I'm yours, and this is our time."

"To love and to cherish," she breathed brokenly, her eyes wild and blazing with ardor. "In sickness and in health . . . all the days of my life. My darling. My darling!"

He soothed her, gentled her, drew her back from the summit, and when she was calm, he began all over again, his voice deep and slow and ardent, his eyes almost black with passion and love as he whispered—explicitly—what he was going to do. And then, with incredible patience and aching thoroughness, with his hands and mouth and his body, he brought her to the point of utter madness, to completion. And she felt her body lifting, rising, flying into the naked sun as the room and the world and reality all exploded into the joy of loving and being loved.

Minutes later, still trembling, she clung to him, her cheek pillowed by his warm, damp chest; his arm holding her; his mouth gently soothing her as it brushed her eyes, her nose, and the curve of her smiling lips.

"I never understood total commitment until you came along," he murmured lazily. "Now it all makes sense. One woman. Children. A home. All of it."

"Don't they say that good girls usually get pregnant the first time?" she asked drowsily, stretching.

He laughed. "You're good, all right," he muttered, turning to loom over her. "Damned good. Come here. . . ."

"But you can't—" she began, until he moved, and she realized that he most certainly could.

"I don't know what kind of books you've been reading, honey," he murmured as his mouth broke hers. "But yes, it's most certainly possible—as you're about to find out. Touch me . . . yes, just . . . like . . . that! God, Maggie!" he ground out, and she

182

yielded immediately as he guided her, prepared her, teased and tormented her in a long, leisurely loving that drove even the time before right out of her mind, until she could do nothing but cling and bite back the urgent cries that whispered hoarsely into his demanding mouth. And she understood finally why the French called it the little death—the most beautiful death imaginable. . . .

The double wedding was a fantasy of white and lace and candlelight, with the church's gorgeous Christmas tree to the right of the altar when Maggie stood with Saxon's ring on her finger, and her sister and new brother-in-law beside them. Tears streamed down her cheeks unashamedly as she acknowledged her husband before the world, her fingers clinging warmly to his, her eyes adoring him.

The organ played, they walked briskly back down the aisle behind Randy and Lisa, and Maggie waved to her father, who was sitting with Sandra, as they left the small church.

"Run for it," Randy told his stepbrother as the well-wishers crowded around and a group of young people moved forward with streamers and tin cans, and the inevitable rice storm began.

Saxon, laughing, prodded Maggie toward his new Ferrari and put her in the passenger side, getting in quickly himself. They barely had time to wave goodbye to Lisa and Randy before they were heading out toward Charleston and their honeymoon.

He clasped her hand warmly in his after he'd turned onto the interstate and they were well out of the thick traffic of the city.

"Happy?" he asked softly.

"Deliriously," she breathed, looking up at him with all her happiness in her face, her eyes. "I love you."

"I love you, my darling. Merry Christmas."

"Merry Christmas." She leaned back in the seat, smiling.

His thumb caressed her palm. "Maggie, it's been six weeks," he reminded her with a laughing sideways glance.

"Yes, I know."

"Well, you little witch?" he prodded. His fingers contracted. "Tell me!"

She turned in the seat and curled one leg under her white satin dress. "I'm sorry, darling," she said gently. "I honestly don't know yet."

"I thought women were supposed to be able to tell."

"Yes, but you're counting your six weeks from the hot tub," she murmured. "I'm counting mine from the rug in front of the fireplace," she added with a blush, remembering that one furious lapse, after which they'd both struggled to keep apart until the rings were in place.

"Ah," he breathed, glancing at her with a wicked light in his eyes. "Talk about stamina. I think I proved mine that night."

"You may very well have proved your virility as well," she said, laughing. "Something that should have happened, hasn't, and it did just after your fall down the staircase."

"You didn't tell me," he accused.

She smiled. "Darling, a woman has to use all her

184

weapons," she reminded him. "I loved you, but I was afraid if I told you, you'd back out of the wedding. At least until that night in the study . . ."

"You little witch," he accused again. "You seduced me!"

"Pot calling the kettle black," she said smugly. "I needed some insurance of my own."

His hand brought hers to his mouth. "Just wait until we get to Charleston," he threatened lovingly.

"I'll do my best, darling," she promised demurely, and her smile held all the promise in the world. "Oh, Saxon Tremayne, I love you shockingly!"

"I love you just as shockingly, Mrs. Tremayne," he replied gently. "What a great many blessings we have to count this Christmas."

"A duke's ransom," she said. She smiled contentedly as she watched the long highway run into the horizon and felt her husband's large warm hand strongly about her own. She wouldn't need presents under the tree this year, she thought joyfully. She already had the best one of all—love.

NEW DELL

CANDLELIGHT
Ecstasy Supreme

TEMPESTUOUS EDEN,
by Heather Graham.
$2.50

Blair Morgan—daughter of a powerful man, widow of a famous senator—sacrifices a world of wealth to work among the needy in the Central American jungle and meets Craig Taylor, a man she can deny nothing.

EMERALD FIRE,
by Barbara Andrews
$2.50

She was stranded on a deserted island with a handsome millionaire—what more could Kelly want? Love.

NEW DELL

CANDLELIGHT
Ecstasy Supreme

LOVERS AND PRETENDERS,
by Prudence Martin
$2.50

Christine and Paul—looking for new lives on a cross-country jaunt, were bound by lies and a passion that grew more dangerously honest with each passing day. Would the truth destroy their love?

WARMED BY THE FIRE,
by Donna Kimel Vitek
$2.50

When malicious gossip forces Juliet to switch jobs from one television network to another, she swears an office romance will never threaten her career again— until she meets superstar anchorman Marc Tyner.

THE SEEDS OF SINGING

by Kay McGrath

To the primitive tribes of New Guinea, the
seeds of singing are the essence of courage.
To Michael Stanford and Catherine Morgan,
two young explorers on a lost expedition,
they symbolize a passion that defies war,
separation, and time itself. In the unmapped
highlands beyond the jungle, in a world
untouched since the dawn of time, Michael
and Catherine discover a passion men and
women everywhere only dream about, a love
that will outlast everything.

A DELL BOOK   19120-3 $3.95

Desert Hostage

Diane Dunaway

Behind her is England and her first innocent encounter with love. Before her is a mysterious land of forbidding majesty. Kidnapped, swept across the deserts of Araby, Juliette Barclay sees her past vanish in the endless, shifting sands. Desperate and defiant, she seeks escape only to find harrowing danger, to discover her one hope in the arms of her captor, the Shiek of El Abadan. Fearless and proud, he alone can tame her. She alone can possess his soul. Between them lies the secret that will bind her to him forever, a woman possessed, a slave of love.

A DELL BOOK   11963-4 $3.95